THE DARKNESS WITHIN

Other Works by Christopher Andrews

Novels

Pandora's Game
Dream Parlor
Paranormals
Hamlet: Prince of Denmark

Screenplays

Thirst
Dream Parlor
(written with Jonathan Lawrence)
Mistake

Theatrical Plays

Duet

Video Games

Bankjob

THE DARKNESS WITHIN

A Short-Story Collection
by
CHRISTOPHER ANDREWS

A Rising Star Visionary Press book
for extra copies please contact by e-mail at
<u>risingstarvisionarypress@earthlink.net</u>
or send by regular mail to
Rising Star Visionary Press
Copies Department
P O Box 9226
Fountain Valley, CA 92728-9226

For Jamie Baxter —
they weren't really your taste,
but you still read them, even
over the phone to Tawnya.

And, as always, for
Yvonne Isaak-Andrews,
my wife, editor, and Imzadi.

CONTENTS

FOREWORD BY THE AUTHOR

Since the release of my first published novel, *Pandora's Game*, people have been asking me how to get their hands on my earlier works. I looked back upon my first outings with a bit of a cringe, but in the end, I felt that my short-stories stood up fairly well. Two of the stories, "Mistake" and "Thirst," were even adapted into independent short-films in 2004 and 2005, respectively.

So, after discussing the matter with my new publishers at Rising Star Visionary Press, we decided to collect the stories together here.

Many fans will be pleased to know that I am including "Connexion," the short-story sequel to *Pandora's Game*. "Connexion" serves as the bridge between *Pandora's Game* and its first novel sequel, *Of Wolf and Man*, which is currently in the works.

Be warned: For those of you familiar with *Pandora's Game*, *Dream Parlor*, *Paranormals*, and *Hamlet: Prince of Denmark*, you will find some of these tales a bit more ... disturbing.

Christopher Andrews
January, 2006

THIRST

(1991)

Sam laced his high-tops tight — a centimeter more and the strings would snap. He had turned an ankle a few months ago and had no desire for an encore performance. Reflector belt in place, he locked his front door, slipped the key into a back pocket, and embarked on his nightly jogging rounds.

Sam Coleman jogged for two reasons: One, his doctor ordered him to get some exercise for his wavering cardiovascular system. Two, it gave him time to work out life's shit.

He breathed deep — in nose, out mouth — the night air. Cool, dry, breezy. Perfect. His legs tightened, then slowly worked into the flow as he left the sidewalk. He'd always heard about avoiding the concrete, but it took his first bout with shin-splints to convince him. A nice, open field ran through the back of his neighborhood. He usually jogged along its outer rim, onto the grassy shoulder by the main street, down a strip of parkway, and back to his house. The forty-five minutes of brain vegetation soothed him, and he definitely needed it now.

He noted absently the old, rusty, chain-linked fence that marked his official starting line. A stinky little pit stewed down the slope to his right, the only drawback to the otherwise pleasant setting. Whatever it was, it had been fenced off and forgotten long ago. He'd signed petition after petition to get rid of it, but the city just didn't care. No public officials were inconvenienced, so fuck the civilians.

Sam didn't care at the moment. His soon-to-be-ex-wife's lawyer had contacted him today. It seemed that, despite their verbal agreement that they would forget alimony, Melissa now wanted to leech off him in his single life as well. Sam'd had his eye on a new Lexus, but he could kiss that goodbye now. To top things off, the office had been a mad house the last week, and—

Sam's right foot suddenly broke through the ground, sinking up to his knee.

Son of a bitch!

His momentum too strong to halt, he pitched forward. His right hand also broke through the weak soil. He rolled out of control down the slope, dirt kicking up into his eyes, his nose, his mouth. He didn't see the fence, the bottom curled up with age, as he passed under it. He fought to brace himself until he finally rolled right into the pit and stopped.

Fuck. He wasn't hurt, but that wasn't the point. He had jogged that route dozens of times and never noticed the ground was weak. He stumbled to his feet, the slime emitting a sickening *shhuuck* as he pulled his butt free. He was bending over to examine his sweat pants when the stench suddenly made him feel lightheaded. For the first time, he was honestly concerned with what the hell this stuff *was*. It smelled like Raid!

With little grace, he crawled on his hands and knees up the hill. No problem, now that he *expected* to deal with it. Wouldn't Melissa just *love* to see him now! Maybe he'd send her this stuff for her next birthday.

Returning home, he removed his sneakers, leaving them outside on the porch, and tip-toed delicately to the laundry room. He stripped, tossed his clothes into the washer, added a ton of detergent, and headed for the shower. If he didn't get this stuff off him soon, with his luck, his dick would probably rot off or something.

Whatever it was, it washed away easily enough. One soaping and he couldn't even smell it anymore. Maybe things weren't so bad after all. He toweled off, threw on his big brown robe, and realized that he was thirsty.

Humming some annoying tune that had been stuck in his head since that morning, he waltzed into the kitchen and opened the refrigerator. He hadn't run long enough to dehydrate, so he nudged aside the thirst quencher and snared a beer. Flipping the tab open, he drew a deep swig as he moved into the living room and switched on the television. Randomly scanning the channels, he found *The Hunt for Red October* on HBO. It was a damn good movie, especially ...

Glancing down at his empty beer can, he grunted in absent surprise — he was still as thirsty as if he hadn't touched a drop.

He crushed the can and tossed it into the trash as he strolled back into the kitchen. Maybe he just wasn't thirsty for beer. Grabbing a cup from the cabinet to the left, he poured himself a tall glass of milk. As it sailed over his tongue and down his throat, he was casually amazed. Even as he drank, even as the liquid washed through his mouth, his thirst wasn't going away. He helped himself to a second glass. No change. Oh, to hell with it! He selected a smaller cup and the orange juice, added a little Vodka, and returned to his lazy chair.

He drank the screwdriver a little more quickly than he'd intended as he continued flipping through the channels. With the things that he'd gone through today, a little persistent thirst was the least of his worries. When a Mountain Dew commercial rolled past, he gave up.

One last glass of water and then to bed with the big thirsty boy!

*　　*　　*

Sam stumbled through the dizzying heat. Every summer, his parents sent him off to this damn camp, and every summer he hated them for it. Masochists that they were, the counselors only enjoyed themselves when going on long hikes in temperatures over one hundred degrees. Unfortunately, they also liked dragging the kids along with them. Of all the things they did, Sam dreaded the hikes the most. The camping wasn't "serious" enough to bring a canteen, and he always got so thirsty ...

So thirty ...

Thirsty ...

*　　*　　*

Sam squinted against the light coming through the window when he awoke. He didn't remember the dream clearly, but he recalled one terrible aspect of it: *Thirst!* He couldn't remember the last time he was this parched! His throat burned, his lips cracked, his tongue swelled, his eyes even itched. He coughed, and cringed against the razorblades that juggled through his larynx. He didn't feel feverish, but if he didn't relieve this thirst immediately he would die!

Snatching his robe only as an afterthought, Sam raced for the kitchen. He grasped the glass he had used for water the night before and hurriedly filled it from the faucet rather than going for the bottled water. He swallowed the fluid in one breath.

It didn't help.

Sam felt fear rising in his gut like the second serving of

water rising in his glass. This was serious — this was *beyond* dehydration.

Gulp!

No relief.

He threw open the refrigerator. His hands closed on the thirst quencher, practically ripped the cap off, and lifted the bottle to his lips. His heart pounded fast as he ingested the entire contents, some liquid spilling down his chin. Dear God, it wasn't helping at all! He hurled the empty bottle away from him, then desperately filled his glass with water once more and drank, for all the good it did him. What was going on—?

The *pit*! Oh God, he'd forgotten about that! That smelly slime had to be involved somehow! He remembered thinking that it smelled like Raid. Wasn't there a rat poison that killed the rodents with a thirst they couldn't slake? For a brief moment he visualized himself standing there drinking water until his stomach burst. He shuddered as he guzzled another glass. If he survived, he would *sue the shit* out of someone for—

The doorbell rang. Damn it, who the hell would come over this early? At this point he didn't care. He couldn't drive himself to the hospital in this condition. He rushed to the door.

Debbie stood outside. How quaint.

Debbie was reason Numero Uno for his divorce and current financial situation. His neighbor for less than a year, Debbie and Sam fooled around on the side for months before Melissa came home and caught them fucking on the living room couch. Debbie pushed hard to be the next Mrs. Coleman — Sam sometimes suspected she'd *arranged* for them to be caught with their pants down, so to speak — but that would happen over Sam's dead body. She'd dressed for this early morning surprise in skin-tight jeans, a white half-shirt — no bra, of course — and bare feet. None of this appealed to Sam. His throat felt like sandpaper. He couldn't say anything, so he gestured her inside.

For reasons unknown, Debbie didn't seem to notice Sam's angst. She murmured some vaguely sexual comment and pawed at him. Trying unsuccessfully to force words through his raw vocal cords, he pushed her away from him, but she obviously thought it was a game. He didn't have time for this! Couldn't she see he was *dying*?!

Then he looked at her, really *looked* her. Her cheeks flushed with passion, her body positively *radiated* before him, tantalizing him. Mesmerized, he reached out and tore away her flimsy shirt. Mistaking this for more foreplay, Debbie let her head fall back as he caressed her breasts, her shoulders, her neck. He felt her pulse against his finger ... and he *knew*.

A little, rational voice screamed from the back of his mind when he realized what he was about to do.

He ignored it.

With animal savagery, Sam dove into her neck, biting ferociously at her jugular. Debbie cried out. She pushed at him, but he held her in a vice grip. Whatever was happening to the rest of him, Sam's teeth were still perfectly normal, so he really had to chew and tear to get through her skin. They stumbled and fell, sprawling onto the floor with Sam on top of her. Debbie struggled for a minute more, then convulsed, then finally lay still. Her blood flowed steadily, and Sam drank deeply.

Oh ... oh ... that's so *much better ...*

At last, he knew what quenched his thirst.

COUNTRY MUSIC
(1991)

Max grumbled as he switched on the windshield wipers. That's all he needed. More rain. Couldn't the damn weather make up its mind?

The sedan splashed through a growing puddle as it coasted along the road. Max hadn't seen another car, much less a cop, for the last half-hour. Of course, it was late, and he was driving through the middle of nowhere. He needed to meet his buddy Alex across the state line before the police hunted him down, but getting lost in the back roads of Arkansas wasn't what he had in mind. The fuel gage registered just over empty, and he hadn't seen any gas station signs for the last fifty miles. To top things off, he'd lost all radio stations except one, and all it played was country shit! Max *hated* country music.

The only things that soothed him were the sacks of money in the trunk ... and the feel of the 9 mm on his lap.

As he rounded a bend — he couldn't call it a "hill"; this whole part of the country was flat as his sister's chest — he spotted a red and yellow neon sign less than a mile away.

Truck stop? he thought hopefully. Maybe his luck was looking up.

His spirits lifted when he realized that it was indeed a truck stop, but they slipped a little when he read the sign:

LEROY'S COUNTRY BUNKER
GAS AND GOOD EATIN'S!

"Terrific," he muttered aloud. What choice did he have? He needed to fill up — his stomach as well as his car. With some reluctance, he pulled into the parking lot. He got out of the car, shoved the gun into the back of his belt, and slipped on his leather jacket to cover it. It would get uncomfortable soon, but he wasn't going anywhere without it. If a cop showed up, he might have to use it. Rain dampened his hair as he trotted to the front door.

The environment assaulted his senses at once. The lights were too bright, the smell of greasy food was too thick, and, worst of all, a jukebox blared a country song much too loud.

"How-deh!" a waitress who was too old and fat called from behind the counter that was too green. "Have uh seat! Ah'll be raht thar!"

Max forced himself to smile as he sat in a booth that was too cushy. The noise set his nerves on edge as the so-called singer howled about his rowdy friends that were coming over tonight. Only two other customers, a couple of hicks sitting across the room, occupied the restaurant — at least he didn't have to listen to *them*. He flipped open the menu and scanned for something to eat. Shit, even the *food* had hick names!

"How are yew this eve-nin'?" the waitress asked as she stepped up to his booth.

"Fine," Max said, resisting the urge to say *fahn*.

"Are yew redy to order?" she yammered, pencil and pad in hand.

"I'd like the ... Cow Burger, please," he said, the stupid name leaving a bad taste in his mouth. "And an ice water."

"Will thaht be ahl?"

Yes, just get the hell away from my table, for the love of God! "Yes, thank you."

Max gritted his teeth as the waitress waddled away. He couldn't do anything to draw attention to himself! This damn music was making him tense — now some guy was telling about living on Tulsa time. His father always listened to this crap, and Max always hated it. Even as a little kid, it ground on his temper until he snapped in every direction. He couldn't afford to let that happen now. Anything that would make him stick in that waitress' mind would be bad news.

His "Cow Burger" — regular hamburger, of course — arrived, and he accepted it with as little discussion as possible, just a "Thank You" to be polite. Ten minutes eating, two at the cash register, another five at the gas pump, and he would be on his way.

The front door kicked in, swinging around and slamming into the wall. A big man stepped in, brandishing a silver six-shooter. He wore steel-toed cowboy boots, Wrangler jeans with leather chaps, a blue-and-black western design shirt, a huge, black cowboy hat with a feather sticking high into the air, and a bandanna, a fucking *bandanna*, across the lower part of his face.

"Ahl raht!" he bellowed in a gruff voice. "Ever one put thar hans in th' air!"

Everyone complied, except Max. A new song had started, one that even Max recognized in spite of himself, the one about a woman named Elvira. Max drew deep breaths as he gripped the sides of the table. Control, control, don't make them remember you ...

"Hay, boy!" the robber yelled as he strutted over to Max. He leveled his gun at Max's temple. "Didn't ah say to put yor hans in th' air?"

"Yes, sir," Max said.

"Then yew better doo it!" He cocked the hammer.

Max slowly lifted his hands from the table top.

"On secon thought," the man said in what Max guessed was supposed to sound like a sly tone of voice, "whah don't yew just han me yor wallet, nass an eezee?" He held out his free hand.

Do it! Max cursed himself. *The real money is in the* trunk. *Your wallet is* nothing! *You don't even have your real I. D. in it.*

Mercifully, for whatever reason, the jukebox skipped at that point and the music stopped. Max felt the tension ease from his muscles.

Thank God, he thought. *I'm going to make it.*

"Doo it *now*, boy!" the man hollered. "Or ah'll blow yew away an they'll hav ta barah yew out yonder!"

Local cemetery, no doubt, Max thought. He said, "Yes, sir." He carefully reached back for his wallet.

The music kicked back in, picking up halfway through another song. Max's ears were besieged by someone yammering about sitting on a front porch and justa swingin'. Adrenaline surged through his veins, his heart thundered, his head pounded. Was he going to let this backward ass country *fuck* take his wallet? *Hell no!*

Max's hand slipped around the handle of his 9 mm. With a quick draw that boggled the shit-for-brains' mind, Max raised the barrel to the man's forehead and fired. The bullet ripped through the back of his skull, raining blood and brain tissue in all directions. Max fired a second time, and the man dropped into a heap on the floor.

The waitress screamed and fainted. The other patrons looked on in shock. The fry cook bolted from the kitchen and snatched the man's fallen pistol.

"Thanks, boy," the cook said. "That wooda bin th' thurd tahm this year." He gave the dead man a little kick in the side. "But whah do yew have uh gun?"

The jukebox was malfunctioning again, so Max had regained control. He could still save himself and get out of here before they called in the town sheriff, or whatever. All he had to say was that he was an off-duty cop and—

The speakers came to life, and Max screamed. It was the country song to end all country songs, the one about the achey-breaky heart!

A red curtain fell behind Max's eyes.

His gun roared to life once again. He fired two shots into the fry cook — one in the face, the other in the chest for good measure. The other customers scrambled to reach the floor, but two more shots ended their miserable little lives. The waitress, who had stirred back to reality, took a single bullet between her mammoth breasts. Max emptied the rest of his fifteen-shot clip into the jukebox until it finally stopped playing.

Max surveyed his work. He had to get the hell out of here! He ripped the six-shooter from the fry cook's hand and ventured back into the rainy night air.

It was their own damn fault, playing that shit!

Max *hated* country music.

BIG LITTLE BROTHER
(1991)

"Have a nice flight?" the taxi driver chit-chatted.

"Yes, thanks," Michael replied.

"Business? Pleasure?"

"Neither, really," Michael said after a moment's consideration. "My parents died. This is the first time I've been home in nine years."

"Oh," the taxi driver said, now uncomfortable. "Sorry to hear that." The man then slipped into merciful silence, leaving Michael to his thoughts.

For the zillionth time that evening, Michael pondered how he honestly felt about all of this — the answers eluded him once again. He loved his parents, but they'd never been close. He had only seen them twice in those nine years, and only because *they* visited *him*. There wasn't any tragic twist of fate that took him away — he'd simply gone off to college and, having discovered a new life, found excuses not to return home. After the third year passed, his father gave up, but his mother still begged him to come home every Christmas, and *that* he *did* regret. The only living person he was coming home to now was his little brother, James. Michael had received the news of his parents' auto accident from his uncle. It surprised him that James hadn't called himself. Granted, he and James had never gotten along, but...

Michael had to smile at himself on that one. To say that

he and his little brother hadn't "gotten along" was the Understatement of the Century. Growing up, Michael had abused James endlessly, calling him his "little little brother" — while Michael reached six feet, one-hundred-seventy by his fourteenth birthday, when Michael last saw James he was still under five feet tall and ninety pounds *tops*, and that was at seventeen years old. Michael cringed when he thought of how terrible he had treated James. When they fought, he took advantage of his size and beat the shit out of James more times that he could count. Maturity brought regret about that, but then, James probably didn't care about it anymore. After all, nearly a decade had passed.

Michael reclined his head against the back of the seat. He'd taken a late flight, and he was tired. Before long, he drifted into a fitful slumber ...

*　　*　　*

James screamed an ear-wrenching war cry as he threw himself at Michael again. Michael laughed, easily dodging the clumsy attack and sending James sprawling to the floor.

"I hate you!" James yelled. He leaped to his feet and kicked at his older brother. Enough was enough! Michael smashed him in the face, wrestled him to the floor of the garage, and sat on him, painfully pinning his arms.

"I'll get you!" James cried, blood running from his busted lip. "I'm going to get big someday and–"

"Oh, shut the hell up, little little brother," Michael mocked. "I'm going away to school soon. By the time you get big, if you ever do, you little runt, it'll be too late. I'll be gone."

James released another scream. With surprising fury, he squirmed so wildly that Michael lost his hold on him. James kicked, and this time his foot landed squarely in Michael's crotch.

"You little shit!" Michael roared. He drove his fist into James' gut. As his little brother gasped for air, Michael decided that he deserved a lot worse. He strode to the metal cabinet and seized an old bicycle chain.

"Oh, no," James whispered as his older brother advanced upon him. "Mike, please, don't."

Michael ignored his pleas as he lashed and lashed and lashed and lashed and ...

*   *   *

"Hey, guy," the taxi driver said. "You're here."

Michael jolted awake. His neck, a neat little crick pinching through its right side, ached in protest. Man, what a dream! The sad thing was it had really happened, the year before he left for college.

Michael mumbled a "thank you," collected his suitcase, paid the fare, and climbed out of the taxi into the muggy night air.

His old home stood before him. The detachment he'd maintained for the last two days collapsed into a puddle of memories. God, why hadn't he visited at least once, *one time* when his mother asked him to? It would have meant so much to her, and cost him so little.

All right, Mr. Pate, he thought, *that road will take you absolutely nowhere. Suck it up and go inside. James probably waited up for you, if he got your message.*

Michael reached the front door, dropped his suitcase beside him, and retrieved his keys. God, so many keys on this ring, and the ones he used the least he'd never bothered removing. Slide the appropriate brown, square-headed key into the lock, a twist to the right, and *voila*!

The smell hit him instantly. In a flash, he recognized the smell of home. Was it the carpet, the walls, the hint of his mother's perfume? He couldn't specify any one thing, but it was definitely *home*.

"James?" he called.

No response. And the lights were all off. Obviously, his little brother had *not* waited up for him, or perhaps wasn't even home. Oh, well.

He moved through the house without flipping any switches; old habits kicking in, he didn't need any light to navigate to his room. He deposited his luggage next to his former bed and crossed the hall to his brother's room.

"James?" he called again. He tried the door. Hmm. Locked. He knocked. "James, you in there? It's Michael." Still no response. Was he here or wasn't he? He knocked again. Nothing.

From another part of the house, Michael heard a distinct *click*. More of a *snap* really, like buttons on a jacket pressed together.

"James?"

He maneuvered back through the hall and entryway to the front door. Distracted by recollection, he'd left it open before, but now it was closed. He reached for the handle but instead bumped his fingers lightly against a wooden bar. His fingers trailed along and touched the padlock securing the bar in place.

What the hell? He reached for the light switch ...

Someone tackled him from behind, driving him forward into the front door *hard*. His breath exploded from his lungs, and his nose exploded across his face. His eyes teared and blood ran into his mouth. Clutching the remains of his nose, he struck at his attacker, but whoever he was, he was big. *Too* big! He felt the person's arms as he was hoisted to his feet — they were like tree trunks! Michael struggled for leverage as the person twisted him around, bent back his arm, and landed a well-placed knee. With an ugly pop, Michael's right shoulder ripped from its socket. He screamed, falling to the floor and curling into a ball, his crushed nose forgotten.

"Long time, no see, Michael," the man said from the shadows. His voice was strikingly familiar.

Through clenched teeth, Michael spat, "Who the hell are *you*?"

The lights switched on. Michael squinted up to see his brother's face on an impossibly large body. Dressed in boots, jeans, a white shirt, and black leather jacket, James looked to be nearly seven feet tall and three hundred pounds *minimum*. Even through the thick jacket, Michael saw bulging muscles flexing and releasing as James glared down at him.

"Recognize me now, Michael?" James said. "It's your little little brother. And I finally got big, Michael."

"James ..." Michael began.

James reached into his leather jacket and produced a long, heavy linked, motorcycle chain.

"Oh, *no*," Michael whispered.

Chain swinging loosely in his hand, James advanced upon him ...

... SUICIDE IS PAINLESS ...
(1991)

I don't want to live.

What do I have to live for? My fiancee dumped me, I flunked out of school, can't get along with my parents, can't get along with my sisters ... I just don't give a shit anymore ... when there's nothing down the road, what's the point in still walking, you know what I mean ...

Swallow this thing here ... supposed to be powerful enough to put me out real quick ... ugh ... the last thing I swallow has to go down crooked, of course ... guess the only thing to do now is wait ...

Should I write a note? Fuck a note, who cares about a note, who am I going to leave a note to ...

... mmm ... this's gotta be the hardest part ... it's done, I took it ... I'm not gonna back down, not gonna call for help ... no one'll find me until Monday morning ... no one's gonna come in here and pump my stomach and save my life ... so, it's done ... but, I'm still here ...

What do you do when you're waiting to die ... well, with the thing I took it's not gonna take too long ... feel sorry for those people who just use sleeping pills ... I wonder how long that would take ... I wonder how long this'll take ...

... hmmm ... it's funny ... here I am sitting here waiting to die, I start noticing sounds I've never noticed before ... the AC adapter in the wall, buzzing ... the refrigerator,

humming ... right now they seem so loud ...

... carpet's dirty ... oh, well, at least I didn't go out with a gun ... be real messed up then, now wouldn't it ...

... I forgot ... I was supposed to call Amy ... wasn't I? ... ha ... oh, well, doesn't matter ... what really matters right now ...

... but I wish I would have taken the time to have one last pepperoni pizza ... that sounds really good right now ...

... wonder what Mom and Dad'll do when they hear ... they'll be upset, I guess ... Mom'll probably cry constantly ... as if she really cares ... shit ... I wonder what Uncle Carl'll say ... I wonder what ... my cousin Mike will say ... God, when was the last time I saw Mike ... musta been ... David's football game ... ha ... God, that was fun, sittin' in the crowd, making all those noises, Mom tellin' us to be quiet, what difference does it make ... maybe I should have left Mike a note ... tell him I'll always treasure the good times ... wherever I'm going I'll treasure the good times ... those football games were fun ... ha, God I'll never forget that kid with the dandruff on his ... shoulders, rootin' for the other team ... I wanted so bad to lean forward n' say "Blue is Better" ... I really should have left Mike a note ...

... oh, shit ... what about David ... fuck, man ... when he was so depressed, I went over there and talked him up   . . . what's he gonna think now ... I mean, there I am, it's kinda hypocritical, isn't it ... I tell him stick it out ...

But it's different for me ... David, I mean, he's got so much to live for, I mean ... where was I ever going ... never did anything right, I got all those ... got all those pictures I drew ... I really wish I coulda gotten those printed somewhere ... now I'll never get the chance ...

... I don't believe I didn't ... get those pictures published ... I always wanted to see those in print ... see the little ... by-line ... "By Mark Anderson" ... oh, fuck ... I'll never see it now ... why couldn't I have at least gotten one before I did

this ... I coulda sent off that last one, that last chance, why didn't I? ... maybe it's not too late ...

What am I saying? It is too late ... I took the damn pill ... I can feel it already, it's ... like a little fuzziness in the back of my head ...

... I wanted to get one drawing published ... just one ... God I'm gonna miss Mike ... Mom's gonna cry ...

... what am I doing ... what am I doing ... David'll feel like I let him down I'll never see Mike again I didn't call Amy back ... Mom'll cry ... all because I gave up, all because I didn't try any longer ...

... how can I give up? ... I always preached to everyone else never give up now I give up ... no, no, no I made a mistake mistake I gotta ... no, I gotta gotta move to ... I've gotta call, fuck, call it's not too late, no it's ... shit, fuckin' room is spinning, man ... no, wait wait wait, it's not too late, I just, gimme time to think, need to think, is this what I want ... I don't, don't have time ... just wanna ... I don't know what ... oh, shit ... I gotta, I gotta gotta get phone, telephone it's fine, I mean it'll be fine, I'll just ... you call 911 ... I'll call 911 emergency and they'll get here ... I mean, they get here fast, right? ... oh, shit! ... legs don't wanna work ... com'on man, come on! ... the damn phone is three feet ... just reach!, okay, okay, be calm ... if you get nervous your heart's gonna beat ... and, uh ... blood supply, will go fast and, you, you die quicker, right? that's how it works, isn't it ... reach fucking phone, just get the fucking phone ...

... can't, I can't see the numbers ... can't no no, come on look ... for God's sake, it's just three numbers, 9 ... 9 ...

... stand up, for God's sake, don't fall down ... up, get up, get up, reach phone God's sake...

I don't want to die, I don't want to die ...

I ... I don't wa ... want to die ...

I ... die ...

...

JUSTICE
(1991)

The radio played easy-listening music as Ruth cruised down the dark highway. The sky was clear and the moon was full, so she didn't bother using the bright lights. She was in no hurry to get anywhere; she was simply enjoying a midnight drive. When she glimpsed the figure on the side of the road, her heart leaped with excitement.

The person, standing with his hand out and thumb erect, was a young man, with neatly trimmed hair, fine clothing, and an expensive-looking backpack. Ah, a bold avenger crossing the country with Daddy's credit card in his back pocket!

Ruth slowed and pulled over, coasting to a stop perfectly beside him. The young man flashed an attractive smile and opened the door.

"Hi," Ruth cooed as the stranger slid into the passenger seat. "What's your name?"

"Seth," the young man replied.

"Nice to meet you, Seth," she said. "I'm Ruth."

With an unnecessary flash of her turn signal, Ruth pulled back onto the road.

"Seatbelt, please," Ruth sing-songed.

With a "Sure," Seth complied.

"Kind of late to be hitching, isn't it?" Ruth said in a teasing tone of voice. "Didn't your mother tell you that's dangerous?"

"Plenty of times," Seth chuckled. "But ... you know how it is. I'm hoping to make the next town by—"

Ruth's left hand engaged the cruise control and her right drifted down to her special little lever. One pull, and Seth's seat fell backward, surprising him as he tumbled back with it. The straight razor flashed in the moonlight as Ruth drew it across his windpipe. Seth gurgled for breath, gripping his throat as blood flowed onto the plastic sheet spread across the back seat. Careful not to hit the jugular — arterial spray would be too messy!

Seth struggled now, clutching at Ruth's arm and the seatbelt buckle that refused to open. The blood bubbled through the gash in his windpipe as he fought to breathe. Ruth calmly waited him out, keeping the car smoothly on the road until he finally laid still.

She smiled as she glanced over at her work. This was one of the neatest jobs she'd done in a long time, maybe *ever*. A little blood to clean off the window, but otherwise the thick, crimson fluid collected entirely on the drop cloth. She would be home in half an hour, and then she could prepare.

She reached her secluded farm house in less time than she'd hoped. Pulling into the barn, she killed the engine and got out. A pull of a chain brought up the lights, and she circled to Seth's side of the car, opening the trunk and retrieving another plastic sheet, this one a bit smaller. She then opened both the front and back doors on Seth's side. Wrapping the smaller sheet around his head and neck, she unlocked the seatbelt with her key and lifted his body from the car. He was a large young man, but Ruth had no trouble. Although petite, she was very strong for her size. She carried the body to her table, then drew water into a bucket and collected her soap, sponges, and towels. She was anxious to get to Seth's body, but first things first! The car must be cleaned right away.

After a quick but necessary scrub down, she at last returned to her latest prize. She meticulously removed his clothing, then examined his body closely. His arms and legs were nice and meaty, his back broad and thick, his chest smooth and solid. Yes, definitely a good hunt tonight. This one would last for some time. Perhaps ... yes, tonight she would have ribs.

Licking her lips, and swallowing as her mouth watered, Ruth picked up her electric steak knife and fired up the generator.

*   *   *

Devin stared into the headlights bearing down on him. He extended his thumb. Maybe this time he would get lucky.

Yes! The car pulled over ten yards in front of him. He jogged up along side of it, but frowned inwardly when he peered through the window.

"Hi," he said courteously. "Thanks for stopping. How far are you going?"

The man driving the car said, "All the way to the state line. Hop in."

"Oh, I'm sorry," Devin said, feigning disappointment. "I have to cut to the west at the exit just a few miles from here. Sorry for the trouble."

"Hey," the man said, "I don't mind taking you that far. Go ahead—"

"No," Devin insisted. "Thank you, anyway."

"No problem," the man shrugged. "Sorry I couldn't help." He waved and drove off into the night.

Devin grumbled. How often did cars come through here this late, and why did they have to go fall through? Things had not been going his way lately!

To his pleasant surprise, another car appeared on the

road only a few minutes later. He extended his thumb again. With his luck, this one probably wouldn't pull over.

But the car did, and he was pleased to see a young blond woman behind the wheel of the little Nissan.

"Hi," she said cheerfully. "Want a lift?"

"Sure do," Devin said, sitting next to her. "Get tired of walking after a while."

"I'll bet." She offered her hand. "I'm Lisa."

"Devin," he returned, shaking her fingers gingerly.

Lisa pressed on the gas and they were on their way. "Where you headed, Devin?" she asked.

"No place in particular," Devin answered.

"Ah. Just wandering?"

"Not exactly." He casually reached into his jacket. "How old are you, Lisa?"

Lisa paused for a second, then said, "Nineteen."

"Young enough for me," Devin said, producing a .357 Magnum.

"Oh, my God," Lisa whispered when she glanced at the gun, her eyes widening in horror.

"Follow the road," Devin said calmly, "then get off at the next exit."

Lisa began crying. "Oh, God, mister, please don't hurt me I swear I'll do anything just please—"

"Do as I told you," Devin sighed, "or I'll blow your fucking head off."

Blubbering and rambling, Lisa did as ordered. Devin guided her off the road and into a secluded clearing.

"Turn off the engine and give me the keys," Devin commanded.

Lisa did.

"Now," Devin said, "slowly step out of the car. If you try to run, I'll kill you."

The two exited the car on their appropriate sides, Devin training the Magnum on her the whole way. Lisa stood still, weeping and trembling, as Devin walked around to stand five feet from her.

"Take your clothes off," Devin said.

Lisa responded by crying even harder.

Devin cocked the hammer. "Strip."

Lisa removed each article of clothing until she stood nude before him. Devin surveyed her body. He had really scored this time. Most women he got were too plump, but this girl, with her shapely legs and firm breasts, could easily make a Playboy bunny. She would do just fine.

"Kneel," he said.

Lisa knelt.

"Close your eyes and open your mouth."

"Oh, God," she whispered, but she complied.

Devin stepped forward, slid the barrel of the gun between her teeth, and fired. Lisa recoiled as if in electric shock, then collapsed. Devin holstered his Magnum, grasped her body, and laid it on the car, her stomach on the hood and her legs hanging to the ground. He pulled the lubricant from his pocket and set it on the hood next to her. He then dropped his pants and began to stimulate himself.

The night was breezy. Her body would cool in no time.

Cool on the outside, but still warm on the inside — just the way Devin liked them.

*   *   *

The Driver spotted the Hitchhiker waiting down the road. The car stopped.

"Hi," the Driver said warmly as the Hitchhiker slid into the passenger seat. "What's your name?"

The Hitchhiker replied, "Devin."

"Nice to meet you, Devin," the Driver said. "I'm Ruth."

With a blink of the turn signal, the car pulled back onto the road.

MISTAKE
(1991)

David playfully kicked a can out of his way as he strode down the path to his apartment. He'd received a positive response to his Public Speaking speech and was in good spirits ... and the fact that it was Friday helped quite a bit, too, of course. He shifted his backpack higher onto his shoulder and climbed the stairs. His eyes were cast downward, so it wasn't until he reached the second-floor landing that he spotted the note taped to his door.

It was on yellow legal-pad paper, folded neatly in half with a big *D* written on it in blue ink. His roommate's name was Bill, so it was a safe bet it was intended for him. He yanked it down and entered.

"Heeey, David!" Bill greeted when he entered. Their two-bedroom apartment was laid out so that Bill's room was to the immediate left of the front door. Bill sat on his bed, a notebook and a copy of *The Great Gatsby* on his lap.

"Heeey, Bill!" David returned. He held up the note. "You know anything about this? I found it on the door."

"Nope," Bill said after a moment's glance. "Probably a love letter from one of your fans."

"No doubt," David chuckled. He crossed through their living room to his bedroom, tossed his backpack onto the floor next to his nightstand, flopped onto his bed, and opened the note.

In large print, it read:

LEAVE ME ALONE

David checked the front for any other markings, then read it again. *Leave me alone*? What the hell was *that* supposed to mean? He considered the note a second longer, then returned to Bill's room.

"What do you make of this?" he asked, handing the note to his roommate.

Bill studied it, performing his own check of both sides. " 'Leave me alone?' "

"Don't ask me," David shrugged. "I just found the thing."

Bill handed the paper back. "A joke?"

"Maybe," David said. He looked the note over one last time, then crumpled it into a ball and tossed it into Bill's wastebasket.

*   *   *

"Call me," the knockout named Rachel whispered with a wink as she handed David her phone number. She stood (thrusting her tits out further than necessary) and walked out of the bar (shaking her butt more than necessary).

"You lucky son-of-a-bitch," David's friend, Anthony, muttered. "Ten bucks says you bed her by the end of next week."

"No, thanks," David said with a smile. "You'd win."

"Oh, you bastard," Anthony groaned.

"Here," David said, tossing him the phone number. "She is *way* too drunk to remember which of us she gave it to. I'll take the next one." He finished the last of his beer and said, "I'm headin' home."

"Make way for Don-fuckin'-Juan," Anthony jeered.

"You safe to drive?"

"Oh, yeah," David said as he thumbed his half of the tab onto the table.

"Uh-huh. See you Monday."

David waved and exited into the cool night air. He *had* gotten drunk last night, then spent his morning nursing a hangover, and he'd had no desire for a repeat performance. Still, it was Saturday night, so he'd been more than willing to share a couple of beers with Anthony. He didn't regret giving up that phone number either; Rachel-the-Theta was a little too gaudy for his taste — all make-up and hair spray. Besides, Anthony only got laid once in a blue moon.

He fished out his keys as he reached his car. He had the gear in reverse before he finally caught sight of the note under his windshield wiper. He rolled down his window, reached out, and snared the piece of paper. Flipping on the interior light, he unfolded the yellow sheet.

I TOLD YOU TO LEAVE ME <u>ALONE</u>

Throwing the door open, David jumped out of the car and swept the parking lot with a suspicious eye. He saw no one, but the hair on the back of his neck rose anyway. He searched a second longer, then slid behind the wheel and headed home.

This was too weird.

*   *   *

The following Monday evening, as David poured over his British Politics notes, the phone rang. Bill was attending his night class, so David rose from the kitchen table and snatched the receiver from its cradle. "Hello?"

No response ... but he heard someone breathing on the

other end.

"*Hello*?" he repeated.

"I know it's you," a female voice said.

"Excuse me?"

"I know it's you," the woman repeated. "And *you* know who this *is*. Don't play *stupid* with me."

"I ... think you have the wrong number," he replied stiffly. "Whom were you calling?"

"I was calling *you*, David. I'm warning you — leave me *alone*." CLICK!

David stood holding the phone for several moments before returning it to its cradle. Notes on his door and car were bad enough, but getting calls and being *threatened* was a whole new ball game. For a chilling second, a line from some old horror flick — *the call came from inside the house* — popped into his mind, but reason quickly shamed him for it. He and Bill only had one phone line, and besides, he would have known if someone else were inside the small apartment.

He lowered himself onto the couch next to the phone. All right, what did he have so far? Some woman knew where he lived, what kind of car he drove, where he hung out, his phone number, and at least his first name. This same person was also accusing him of ... *something*, and she wanted to be left alone. Did this warrant calling the police? He hadn't really been spooked until this phone call, and even now he would be hard pressed to call it *fear* — "the creeps" maybe, but certainly not *fear*!

Returning to the kitchen table, David forced his attention back to British Politics.

*   *   *

David hummed in sync with the music as the water

cascaded over his head. He had an early class on Wednesdays, so he washed his hair Tuesday nights rather than the next morning. The stereo blared from the living room, as Bill had gone to the Kettle to study and would not be bothered. David swayed to the motion as he rinsed the shampoo from his hair.

Stepping from the shower, he wiped the mirror clear and glanced at his wet hair. He picked up the cutting shears and clipped a touch at the hair over his ears. He held them poised in front of his bangs for just a moment, then set them down again. The last time he tried that, he had to wear a baseball cap for two weeks — let his barber deal with those annoying cowlicks.

As he towel-dried his hair, the music suddenly stopped. He paused for a moment, then glanced at his watch on the counter. He hadn't expected his roommate back for hours.

"Bill?" he called.

No answer.

Wrapping the towel around his waist, he opened the bathroom door. He glanced around the living room but found nothing disturbed. Judging from the display lights, the CD player was still on, but the volume had been turned all the way down.

"Bill?"

Nothing.

Moving cautiously now, he strode to Bill's room — lights off, backpack missing, jacket gone from the back of the chair.

Whoever had turned down the music, it had *not* been his roommate.

David panicked at first, spinning around his apartment and whipping his head back and forth. Then he got bold and yelled halfhearted challenges as he threw open the closet doors and peered into every conceivable hiding place. His heart thundered and adrenaline fired into his veins in excess.

The phone rang. David yelped, then, angry with himself for his unwitnessed display of nerves, he charged at the phone and snatched the receiver.

"Hello?!" he snapped.

"Hello, David," said the expected voice.

"Who the fuck do you think you *are*?!" he demanded. "I don't know what—!"

"What's the matter?" she interrupted. "You don't mind torturing me. Don't you like it when I return the favor?"

"What the *fuck* are you—?!"

"Calling me at all hours. Spying on me. Following me. I told you to leave me alone, and I *meant* it."

"Listen, you crazy bitch—!"

"*Paybacks* are a bitch," she corrected, then hung up.

David stood naked in his living room — he'd lost the towel in his mad race around the apartment — holding the phone and breathing heavily.

call the police

This had gone too far! Sneaking in *and out* of his apartment ...

call the police

No. If that bitch thought she was going to get the better of him, she had another think coming!

don't be proud, David, call the police

The front door was still locked, and she couldn't have locked it behind her. She must have crawled up onto the balcony and come in through the french doors.

David, you idiot, CALL - THE - POLICE!

Well, he would just go to bed early tonight, and maybe snuggle up with his baseball bat to boot!

POLICE!

"No!" He'd deal with this on his own.

* * *

mmmph mllli umm

David stirred slightly. His thoughts focused lazily as the fuzziness of sleep receded. Oh, damn, he'd drifted off. Lucky for him that crazy bitch hadn't—

The hair rose on the back of his neck again. He was lying on his stomach, his head facing the wall away from the rest of the room. In the darkness he could barely see his aluminum bat peeping out from under the covers. Behind him, he picked up the faintest movement, detected more by intuition than by his ears. A light brush, like a foot against carpet. Bill would never come into his room without knocking first.

David's right hand snaked out toward his bat. When the comforting metal was just a centimeter away, another hand closed on his wrist. David screamed as his cutting shears pierced the back of his hand, thrusting through his palm and into the mattress. He tried to rise, and something thick and fuzzy — something distinctly like the terrycloth belt of his robe — flashed over his head and tightened around his throat. His right hand, the looped ends of the scissors still protruding like antennae, ripped free from the mattress as he was jerked from the bed.

As his line of vision passed by his mirror, David glimpsed the woman behind him. She was short and petite, disguising the amazing strength she clearly possessed. She whipped him around and thrust him through the door of his bedroom. Two steps, and he was sprawled on his stomach on the kitchen table. The woman leaped on top of him, maintaining her firm grip on the choking belt, but allowing him to breathe just enough to stay conscious.

"You just wouldn't let it lie, would you, David?" she whispered into his left ear. Her breath was hot and fetid. "I warned you and warned you, and you still wouldn't let it lie."

Even if David had *wanted* to respond, he wouldn't have been able. He was vaguely aware of the growing pool of blood from his right hand, and that it was wetting his hair.

"How many women have you done this to, David? How long did it take you to pick the wrong one, to pick *me*?"

David struggled for air.

"You'll never do it again, David."

The woman pulled hard on the belt, and David's already constricted air passage sealed shut. With a final, desperate burst of energy, David heaved back, going with her pull. She slipped the barest amount, but it was enough. As strong as she was, David still outweighed her by at least fifty pounds.

They rolled off the table and onto the floor. David landed sideways on top of her, and her knee slammed into his ribs, cracking at least one. He twisted around to face her, but her choke-hold held. Reaching out with his right hand, he covered her face so that the scissor blades jutting out of his palm touched her left eye.

This is gonna hurt.

With his left hand, David slammed the handles down with all his might. Had his throat not been cut off, he would have screamed again. The woman shuddered, but eerily held her silence. A second hit, and only the ringed tips of the handles showed from the back of his hand. The length of the blades passed through his palm and her eye and stabbed into her brain. She tightened the choke for a brief instant, then relaxed.

Coughing, David used his free hand to pull the belt from his neck. He soon found that pulling his hand off her face was a much harder task. He almost blacked out from the pain, but he couldn't bear the thought of remaining stuck to her in that way.

As he fumbled for the phone and the light, he gaped at

the woman, getting a good look at her for the first time. She was one of his neighbors! He had seen her occasionally for months! She lived in the building across from his. What in *the hell*—?!

Seizing control of himself, and gritting his teeth against the pain in his side and the scissors that maintained their invasion of his body, David dialed 911.

*   *   *

Anthony strode through the hospital. The police officers passed him going the opposite direction, but he ignored them. He made his way to the room where Bill sat beside David's bed.

"Hey, man," David said through a pain-killer haze.

"Jesus, David," Anthony said as he eyed the huge bandage on his friend's right hand. "I came as soon as I heard. What the hell happened?"

"We just found out ourselves," David said. "Grab a seat. When my parents get here, I won't get a word in edgewise."

Anthony sat in the not-so-comfortable chair opposite Bill. David's roommate merely sat and listened as he spoke.

"You remember that note I told you about Saturday night? Well, it didn't end there. Last night, the crazy bitch who *wrote* that note got into my apartment and attacked me. I ... killed her in self-defense."

"Oh, man," Anthony muttered.

"Tell me about it," David chuckled. "Anyway, the police just filled me in on the big picture. This lady, a neighbor of mine, just got out of a *mental institution*. Treated for years for *paranoia*. Guess she wasn't cured, 'cause she accused *me* of harassing *her*. She told her co-workers about this young guy in her apartment complex who kept calling her and telling her that he was watching her. And *my* apartment just happened to be across from hers. Lord only knows how she got my name, but she decided to return the favor."

Anthony released another, "Oh, man."

David half-shrugged. "You know, in a weird sort of way, I'm *glad* she turned out to be *nuts*. I mean, if someone really *had* been harassing her, I'd hate to think that she did this to me *by mistake*."

*   *   *

The next day, Bill slipped his key into the mail box. Hmm, nothing but junk mail today! As he flipped through the assembled envelopes addressed to "Resident," he glanced along at the other boxes' names and numbers.

Ah, there.

Returning to his apartment, Bill tossed the mail onto his bed, picked up the phone, and dialed information.

"City, please."

He named his own.

"Yes?"

He asked for the residential number of one Pamela Stevens.

The recording clicked into play. "The number is ..."

Bill memorized it with practiced ease. He pressed his thumb over the connection button and moved to the window. Adjusting the blinds, he sat on his bed and looked across, not like he did last time, but at a new angle. While looking, he dialed the number and lifted the receiver to his ear.

Ring. Ring. Ri—

"Hello?"

"Hello, Pam. I'm watching you right now..."

YOUR COMMAND IS MY WISH
(1991)

Andrew kicked himself mentally as Trevor Stevens kicked him physically. He'd known for weeks that Alison Walker had broken up with Trevor, but he'd also known that Trevor wasn't accepting it. Still, like the fool he was, like the fool he had always been, Andrew reached for the stars and asked Alison out on a date.

The results: Not only did Alison laugh in his face, but Trevor was now beating the shit out of him for his "fucking nerve."

Blood filled his mouth from the gash in his lip and the chunk missing from his tongue. His left eye was already swollen shut, and he felt sure that last kick had broken his collarbone. Still, even Andrew Thurmond had his pride, and he refused to cry out as the varsity wrestler pommeled him.

With one last kick, and a good hunk of spat mucus, Trevor towered over Andrew and said, "Stay the hell away from Alison, Thurmond. The next time I see you anywhere near her, I will kill you ..."

* * *

Bzz! Bzz! Bzz!

Andrew grimaced as his alarm clock sounded the beginning of a bright new day. He grumbled, rolled over in his bed, and slapped the snooze button. He wanted to fall back asleep for the allotted time, but the dream had disturbed him beyond slumber. The episode had occurred the year before, and each time he considered asking someone out, The Lesson Of Alison Walker pushed its way from the depths of his subconscious. Mandy Peterson, the new girl in his History class, was attractive and had many friends. What would she want with a nerd who had nothing, not even the stereo-typical genius I. Q.? Granted, she didn't have an ex-boyfriend like Trevor Stevens — who graduated last spring, much to Andrew's relief— but could he risk the humiliation of being turned down for the zillionth time in his fifteen years?

The alarm buzzed again. So soon? He must have drifted off after all, although it was a fitful doze at best.

He again punched the snooze, but this time he sat up.

Maybe this should be the day, he pondered. *Maybe I should get it over with and ask Mandy to go out with me.*

The consideration was promptly followed by a crushing wave of anxiety so intense that for a moment Andrew thought he might faint, or vomit, or both.

"I can't go on like this," he whispered aloud in self-pity. *Jerry's always saying I'm too hard on myself. Maybe he's right. Maybe I should just do it.*

His nerves were so high strung from this inner debate that Andrew actually yelped when the alarm shrieked a third time.

"Andrew!" his mother's gruff, cigarette-roughened voice called from the other room. "Get your ass out of bed and shut off that goddamn alarm! If I'm late again because of your lazy butt there'll be hell to pay!"

Andrew switched off the alarm and hastily dressed for school.

"I don't work two goddamn jobs for my health ..." his mother's voice faded as she walked to the other end of their cheap apartment.

Despite the verbal fusillade, Andrew's fingers slowed as he buttoned his shirt. He drew a slow, deep, shaky breath ... then did something he had not done in a long time.

He got down on his knees and prayed.

Dear Jesus in Heaven, he began, and shuddered against such a formal commencement. *Jesus,* he started over, *I know I've never been quite the Christian that Father Gardener says we should all be, but I'm hoping You'll hear me anyway. I'm stuck, Jesus. I've never been much of anybody ... I'm sure You know ... but it's been so much worse since The Lesson Of— since the Alison Walker thing ...* His sweaty hands clasped so tightly the knuckles turned white. *I ... I need to* know*, Jesus. I need to know if it will ever be* any *better than this. I ... I'm going to ask Mandy out on a date today. Not to fornicate!* he added hastily. *Just ... just to know. To know if I'm worth it. So, please, if I am* worth *anything anymore, please help me get through this.*

"Goddamn it, Andrew!"

"Amen," he finished, then rushed out to meet his mother.

*   *   *

"Hey, Andrew," Jerry said as he sat in the chair next to the Sophomore. "How you doin'?"

Andrew washed the bite of hamburger down with his iced tea, holding up a finger for Jerry to "wait a second." Jerry Hill, the only person in the school — of any popularity — who ever treated him like a human being, often joined him briefly for lunch. Jerry ate with his other friends, of course, but Andrew appreciated the gesture.

"Okay," Andrew said when his mouth finally cleared. "I'm a little nervous."

"What about?"

"I have History next hour," Andrew explained. "I, uh, I'm ..." He hesitated. Should he say anything to Jerry? Caution and jumping nerves warned against it, but since his morning prayer, his resolve and — despite past experience — his growing confidence had also created a touch of enthusiasm and *excitement* ... excitement which he now decided that he wanted to *share*. "I'm going in early to ask out the new girl, Mandy Peterson," he announced.

Jerry started. "Andrew, I wouldn't do that, buddy."

Andrew blinked. "Why?"

"I hate to tell you," Jerry said sincerely, "but she already has a boyfriend. He goes to another school."

To say that Andrew's hopes crumbled and burned would have been an understatement. His gaze shifted from Jerry's face to focus blankly on the table.

"Andrew?" Jerry asked. "You okay?"

Andrew paused for a second, then said, " 'm fine."

"Sorry to be the one to disappoint you," Jerry said, giving him a sympathetic pat on the shoulder. "I've got to go. Maybe next time, huh?"

Andrew mumbled something unintelligible as he stood and walked away from the table.

Jerry sat and stared after him for a moment, feeling as though he just told some two-year-old that Santa Claus was all make-believe. He felt bad, all right ... but confident that he had done the right thing. Mandy Peterson really *did* have a boyfriend at another school. Sure, the inside scoop was that the two of them were on the verge of breaking up, but what difference could that really make? Andrew was nice, but he was ... well, he was a *nerd*. Jerry was reasonably sure that Mandy would have just laughed in Andrew's face, and after the Alison Walker thing last year ... the poor kid had been through enough.

Shaking his head in pity, Jerry hurried to join his waiting group of friends.

*   *   *

So, this is the way it's going to be. Fine.

Trudging home from school, Andrew thought this and similar proclamations, over and over again.

I got my hopes up. It's my own fault. My own fault for ever thinking I *could possibly* amount *to anything. I'm a* victim, *that's all. A loser, a nobody, and a* victim, *now and forever and ever, amen.*

Amen ...

Andrew had not really felt pain and upset per se at Jerry's terrible revelation — the aching *emptiness* had run too deeply to allow for such trite emotions. Andrew was now a *void* — a void that could surely never be filled ...

Amen ...

As he passed by the town's older library, his stride faltered. His eyes turned toward the aged, ugly, but well furnished structure of knowledge.

Amen.

That morning, he had sought strength and comfort, and it had been *denied* him. But perhaps there was *another* place he could turn for the strength.

Andrew deviated from his usual, homeward path. And as he approached the old building, the void began to fill after all.

It filled with anger, and *hate* ...

*　　*　　*

Andrew lit the candle, and eased back on his haunches, a satisfied, *twisted* grin on his face.

All around him, every text on voodoo, black magic, and the occult the library had offered littered his room floor. Maybe he wasn't a *genius*, but he *was* a fairly quick study. He'd found a hex (spell? feit? whatever) that promised to bequeath *instant power* to those determined and true, and the ingredients for the potion had been so simple, so basic and common, that he had located most of them around the apartment. The rats' eyes had been the most exotic and grotesque, but after half-an-hour out by the complex dumpsters, he had those, too.

Now he held the brown and noxious mixture in a tin cup over the candle's flame, counting down from sixty to zero in his head.

Instant power. Yes. That's what he needed. *Power.*

Finishing his countdown, he blew on the concoction to cool it and stumbled through the words.

"Dlog Bat-nap Tilop Uol."

(Haitian? Greek? Latin? did it matter?)

Steeling himself, he drank the fluid down. It didn't taste as bad as it smelled, although the soap shavings did seem to stick to his tongue.

Instant power.

Thrusting the cup away from him, Andrew gazed down in expectation at his frail arms.

Nothing. Still as frail as ever.

Andrew frowned. *No ...*

He flexed his muscles, expecting, *hoping*, they would ripple with new, barely contained thunder.

Nothing. Zip.

Slowly, something akin to panic began to rise within

Andrew.

No, no, no. Instant power. Instant!

Andrew drew the book closer, reread the instructions, then knocked the book aside. As the text flipped over, a passage written on the backside caught his attention for the first time. His eyes tearing and lower lip quivering, he read:

PUBLISHER'S NOTE:
The list of "spells" contained herein,
while reportedly derived from actual
"research," should be strictly considered as
and read for entertainment only.

Idiot. Idiot, idiot, idiot!

Andrew threw the book across the room and cried in earnest. *Loser*! He was such a fucking *loser*! "Instant power?" Ha! Andrew was about as capable of ever having true power as ... as ...

I DRANK RAT EYES!

Running to the bathroom, Andrew promptly heaved the "potion" back up into the toilet.

Finally, destitute, he returned to his room and collapsed onto the floor. His vacant gaze focused on the candle.

"I'm nothing," he started to say, but the words merely emerged as strickened grunts through vocal cords that tingled tremendously. Side-effects of his Instant Power Potion, no doubt.

Slowly, his hand sought and located the razor blade he had used to shave the soap. Where had he ever gone wrong? Surely people weren't *born* losers. What had he done along the way to foul up his every sense of acceptability, of what was cool to say, wear, or do, and what was not? He felt the sharp metal between his finger tips. His mother would not get home from work until after midnight. There would be no saving him. At least one thing he had in common with everyone, with no exception, was that *everyone* dies.

With firm resolve, he placed the razor against his left wrist ...

*   *   *

Andrew's eyes snapped open when his mother slammed the garage door. In a daze, he looked around his room. The candle had burned down to almost nothing. The clock read twelve-thirty-four, but that was impossible. Mere moments ago he was about to ...

The razor blade, still poised to cut, rested against his wrist, a mere drop of dried blood on its tip. Had he blacked out, only to sit frozen for the time he needed to end his life? But his muscles weren't even stiff! What ... couldn't he even commit *suicide* without fucking it up?!

His bedroom door opened and his mother, waitress uniform on and cigarette hanging from her lips, entered. He'd asked her countless times not to smoke in his room, but she heeded his request no better than she noticed the razor blade in his hand.

"Andrew," she began, "how many times have I told you to take out the goddamn garbage on Mondays? And what is this goddamn mess—"

Andrew, his nerves and confusion rising to a peak, screamed, "*Shut up!*"

Instantly, his mother closed her mouth. She stared at him in disbelief. Groaning inwardly, Andrew prepared himself for an explosion, but it never came. To his surprise, his mother merely stood her ground, her face straining in anger, but not saying a word. Her behavior baffled him. He hated to look a gift horse in the mouth, but why wasn't she screaming at him for talking back? She was acting as if ...

... as if she *couldn't* say anything.

"Mom?" he said cautiously. "Are you all right?"

His mother's face reddened further and she flapped her arms — she looked like a chicken, but he felt no urge to laugh — but she still said nothing.

"Mom?" He stood, casually setting the razor blade on his nightstand, and approached her. "What's wrong?"

She opened her mouth halfway, but no words came out. She shook her head violently, then drew back to strike him.

"Mom! What did I—"

Her hand swung about, aimed at his face.

"*Stop!*" he cried, throwing his arms up and scrambling back.

When he felt and heard nothing, he lowered his arms and stared at his mother. She stood frozen like a statue, her blinking, horror-filled eyes the only indication that she was alive. What was going on? He carefully stepped forward again. She did not move. Why ...

With slow realization, Andrew thought about the exact words he'd spoken — how they almost vibrated his entire throat — and what he had then witnessed. Could ... what ... but that was impossible! Wasn't it?

"The list of 'spells' contained herein, while reportedly derived from actual 'research,' should be considered as and read for strictly entertainment only."

"actual 'research' "

"Say something," Andrew said.

His mother uttered the word, "Something," and nothing more.

A real response, he wondered, or sarcasm? He said, "Talk to me."

Immediately, his mother's mouth flew into motion, although her body remained in the same rigid pose. "Andrew, what the hell are you doing to me when I get my hands on you how dare—"

"Shut up," Andrew stated nonchalantly.

Her mouth again sealed.

Andrew sat on his bed to think about what was happening.

Dlog Bat-nap Tilop Uol ...

"Actual 'research' " indeed.

Andrew knew his mother well enough to know it wasn't a joke, but if what he thought was happening really *was* happening ...

"Sit down," Andrew said.

She did, right on the floor.

Instant power.

And so began a long night of experimentation.

*   *   *

Andrew arrived at school late the next morning. He had left his assignments and school books at home — he no longer needed to deal with those. His footsteps echoed through the empty halls as he headed for the principal's office. He heard the muffled chatter from the rooms he passed, and he smiled.

"Hey," Mr. Taylor, one of the assistant principals, said when he rounded a corner and spotted Andrew. "You should be in class, son. What's your name?"

Andrew regarded the old man, his gut bulging, his hairline receding, his mustache too thick. Mr. Taylor had never particularly bothered him. He would go easy on this one.

"Don't move."

Mr. Taylor stopped in his tracks, his body paralyzed in mid-stride. He stared at Andrew in horror. Andrew merely smiled and continued on his way.

Andrew entered the office. One of the three secretaries glanced up as he moved behind the desks toward the intercom system. "May I help— Young man, you aren't allowed—"

"Be quiet and don't move," Andrew said, "that goes for all of you."

The two women and the man obeyed perfectly. Andrew needed them silent for his experimentation. If this didn't work, he would have to adjust his plans.

Flipping the switch on, he spoke into the microphone. "Shout once." The building trembled as over a thousand students, teachers, and janitors yelled in unison. Andrew heard the brief racket, and he was pleased.

The Voice was transmittable. Everything was working out perfectly.

Over the intercom he said, "Do not leave this building. Do not contact anyone outside this building in any way, shape, or form. Do not speak over a whisper, and do not move any faster than a slow walk. Do not attempt to harm Andrew Thurmond in any way, directly or indirectly. Do not come within ten feet of Andrew Thurmond without explicit instructions." He reached into his pocket and withdrew a rumpled sheet of paper, a list of everyone he could think of who had ever hurt him. "The following people will gather in the study hall ..."

*   *   *

Jerry Hill, moving at a slow grind (at least, his *feet* moved slowly — his thoughts, and *heart*, raced like a stallion), made his way to the study hall. Andrew had not included him in the list of over two hundred people, but he hadn't told him to stay away, either. Hours had passed, and it was clear what was happening — everyone was terrified.

No one on the outside had discovered the problem yet, but it was only a matter of time before Mr. and Mrs. Smith wondered why Little Johnny wasn't home for supper. Unfortunately, Jerry believed that *he* was the only chance they had, and damn if his sense of responsibility wasn't working at full steam. He opened the study hall door ...

Dear God ...

The sights Jerry saw as he crossed through the study hall were horrifying beyond his darkest nightmares. Moans of pain filled the air, but only at an eerie hush.

Todd Parker, a druggie who once broke Andrew's pinkie, sat on a table twisting each of his own fingers until nothing but skin held them onto his hand. Since he could not use his destroyed left hand on his right, he was using his teeth as a vice ...

A football player — Jerry recognized his face, but could not recall his name — whimpered as he repeatedly wiped Bengay into his eyes ...

Marcie Jackson pulled her hair out, ten strands at a time...

Terry Keech broke a piece of plywood over his knees, then jammed the splinters under his fingernails with all of his might ...

Darrell White pounded himself in the groin with a baseball bat, and Jerry could already see a blood stain forming on the crotch of his jeans ...

Jerry fought to keep from screaming as he approached Andrew's side of the room.

Hold it together, Jerry. Just hold it together. You don't have the luxury *of freakin' out.*

" ... will hold your breath," Andrew was saying to a tall girl Jerry didn't recognize, "until you pass out, then breath normally until you wake up, then hold your breath again. Repeat the process until I say otherwise. Do this ... oh, over there."

The girl, her face already distinctly blue, marched off. Jerry trembled inside as Andrew turned to face him.

"Jerry!" he exclaimed. "What are you doing here?"

"I wanted to talk to you, Andrew," Jerry said. The younger boy's casual demeanor frightened him more than anything else.

"I'd love to," Andrew said, "but I'm sort of busy at the moment. Actually, you've arrived just in time! I'm going into a new phase."

New phase? Jerry wanted to ask, but he was too afraid to form the words.

Andrew craned his neck, looking around the room, then smiled. "Alison Walker! Come over here!"

Jerry glanced back at the beautiful girl as she approached, and he groaned inside. Everyone remembered the incident from last year with Trevor Stevens. He could only imagine what Andrew had in store for Alison, who indirectly caused the beating.

Andrew stood before Alison. "Do not move," he told her. She gazed at him in fear as he circled her, surveying her body.

"Andrew ..."

"Just a second. Alison, take off your clothes." As she did as instructed, Andrew regarded Jerry with a hint of impatience. "What is it, Jerry?"

"Andrew," Jerry forced the words through his dry throat, "I don't understand what is going on, but ..."

"It'll have to wait, Jerry," Andrew said as Alison finished undressing.

"Andrew—"

"Be quiet, Jerry."

Jerry, of course, found that his vocal cords no longer functioned. Rather than risking further commands, Jerry withdrew a safe distance to wait his turn and, sadly, looked away.

"All right, Miss Walker," Andrew said. "For starters, take *my* clothes off ..."

*   *   *

An hour later, after Andrew satisfied himself with an Alison Walker / Mandy Peterson combination and needed a break, he summoned Jerry to him, and gave him permission to speak.

"Andrew," Jerry said oh-so-cautiously, "I don't know how you're doing this. It's, uh, really quite impressive."

"Mm-hmm."

Jerry swallowed hard. "I, uh, was wondering, how long this was going to go on?"

"Well, let's see," Andrew answered, his play at deep thought heavy with sarcasm, "I'm fifteen years old, multiply that by a factor of, oh, I don't know, *one thousand*."

"Andrew," Jerry whispered, "please. On ... on behalf of everyone in here right now, I-I beg you for mercy."

" 'Mercy,' huh? Really? And how much fucking *mercy* did these goddamn motherfuckers ever show *me*? *Huh*?!"

Jerry did not respond directly — they both knew the answer to *that*. Instead, he said, "But that's not really a *viable comparison*, is it? I'm the first to admit that you've had a pretty shitty life, Andrew, but when did these people *ever* do anything like *this* to you? To *anyone*?"

Andrew's gaze was frigid. "Be very careful, Jerry. It's only because you were nice to me that you've made it this far."

That's it, Jerry, just walk away get away from him let him do whatever the hell he wants it's not your responsibility the monster's not even human *anymore*

"Think about it, Andrew," Jerry pressed on, his stomach tight and cold and his hands clammy. "Where does it stop? How long can this go on? How much longer before people outside come—?"

"I'll take care of them when that happens."

"Then just think, really *think* about what you're doing here. Sweet Jesus, Andrew—"

"Jesus doesn't care. He had a chance to stop this. He probably *wanted* it to happen this way—"

Jerry Hill had never been the most devout Baptist. He rarely attended church anymore, except for Easter and Christmas morning. But he'd been raised *consistently* enough that the sheer *blasphemy* of Andrew's words shocked, appalled, and, to his misfortune, momentarily seized over his better judgement. That, coupled with the high tension of his frayed nerves, pushed him over the edge.

Jerry snapped.

"How dare you! Jesus should strike you down, you evil little bastard! Thousand fold, my ass! You are a thousand times worse than anybody who ever crossed your path, and that includes TREVOR FUCKING STEVENS!"

There was a silent moment that nonetheless seemed to *echo* through the study hall — even the moans of anguish ceased for a beat. Jerry's avouchment had touched the old Andrew, the small Andrew who cowered when his mother — God rest her soul — would so much as clear her throat.

Then the moment passed ... and Jerry felt his nuts sink. Andrew's eyes tightened in anger until they were nothing more than tight slits, and when he spoke, his throat vibrated even more than usual.

"Eat shit, Jerry."

Jerry's face reddened as he strained for the bowel movement necessary to follow the order. Andrew snorted, and turned back to Alison and Mandy with renewed vigor.

*   *   *

The idea struck Andrew on the third day. After obtaining a megaphone from the athletic department, Andrew had no trouble holding the outside authorities at bay when they finally arrived the first night — he figured he had *at least* a week before he needed to worry about an *air strike* or anything of *that* sort. The only lasting visage of Jerry Hill's denouncement was the mention of the one person Andrew would like to revenge himself upon more than anyone else — Trevor Stevens. He wanted just the right touch, and he now thought he had it.

To test his idea, he ordered a corpse from the town morgue brought to him at the school. As the body lay before him in the study hall, he addressed it.

"Live."

The corpse opened its eyes, spasmed, and collapsed. With its veins filled with embalming fluid instead of blood and its guts eviscerated, it could not live beyond the first second, of course, but it still served its purpose.

Andrew now knew that his power extended even beyond the grave ...

*   *   *

Trevor Stevens raged at his compulsive, unexplainable behavior. He had received a call in his dorm room the day before, a male voice saying a simple, "Return to your old high school at once. Come to the study hall," and he was damned if he wasn't doing just that. He did not know why, but despite his efforts, he could not prevent himself from driving non-stop until he reached his home town, and Blackwell High.

Leaving his truck running, he strode through the parking lot, past the immobilized police officers and media, and into the school. When he finally stepped into the study hall, his body was again his own. He glanced about himself. The lamps were off, and only the street lights flowing through the windows lit the large, shadowy room. He smelled a myriad of odors, ranging from vomit to excrement to the scent of sex. What in the hell—?

"Come here," a voice said in the dark. Once more, Trevor cursed as his body became a puppet, striding steadily toward the source of the command. A lone figure waited on the far side of the room, and it wasn't until Trevor stood directly before him that he recognized the boy.

"*Thurmond*?!" he stammered. "What the fuck is this?!"

Andrew grinned at his old tormentor, but said nothing.

"Listen, you little shit!" Trevor grunted through clenched teeth. "I want to know what's going on, and I want to know right—"

"Trevor Stevens," Andrew said, "*go to Hell.*"

Game Reincarnate

(1991)

The King turned to his wife. Now, as ever before, his heart of hearts leaped at the mere sight of her beauty. Her grace, the smooth curves of her body, the beautiful ivory of her skin. If ever was crafted the finest Queen, she stood beside him now.

"My lord," she pleaded, "my love, tell me we must not face this horrid contest again."

"Be strong, my wife," he said with firm resolution. The conviction of his voice offered her some support, at least for the time being. "You know our fate. This is far from the first, and it will not be the last."

The Queen nodded. She knew he spoke the truth. Perhaps this battle, at least, would end well. Had she been able, she would have touched his arm with a gentle hand. She regarded those around them. They were flanked by fine warriors. Foremost, of course, were the three sets of twins; Bruce and Blake, Knicholas and Knathaniel, and Robert and Roman. Accompanied by the many nameless foot soldiers, they were a formidable fighting force. But she also knew that their enemy matched them power for power. Only skills changed, only skills mattered.

The King said, "It is time," and the Queen resisted the chill that threatened her spine. She needed strength for what must be done.

Their army shot into formation, foot soldiers making way for Bruce and Blake as they leaped to an offensive posture. The enemy – damn their ebony hearts – countered with terrifying ease. K nicholas guided his steed forward to reinforce Bruce's position, then pressed his attack.

Far across the field of battle, the King glimpsed his opposite number shuttling to the right swifter than normal. The King knew the secret to his nemesis' maneuver, but chose not to emulate it.

K nathaniel surged forth on his stallion, mirroring his twin's earlier strategy. Unfortunately, he realized his mistake too late. Seizing the opening he had provided, one of the enemy's special warriors sailed in, slaying a foot soldier and placing the King in personal jeopardy. A moan escaped his lips as he shamed himself for such amateur planning.

Far from helpless, the King disposed of the threat with relative ease. Another enemy drew dangerously close, forcing the King to retreat a step. In the exchange, K nathaniel fell to the rival queen. A foot soldier almost snared her, but she withdrew far from the simpleton's reach. Roman strode to his King's side to adjust for their losses.

The enemy gave no quarter. The Queen evaded an impending attack, only for Blake to fall and the King to face further peril. A foot soldier slew the threatening Knight, but in turn died at the other-queen's hands. Roman tried to take better position, but the second black knight ended his life.

"Pull together!" the King bellowed, his lost men tugging at his heart even as this slaughter nagged at his keen mind. "We are falling apart too quickly! Fight! Fight to your dying breath!" Even as he cried out, Knicholas expired.

The King pressed hard for an offensive move, but failed miserably. Before his tearing, saddened, disbelieving eyes, his wife, the Queen, fell to her dark opposite.

"No!" he wept, but he had no time for misery. Victory, and his life, were at stake.

Bruce returned to the home front to assist his liege, but the King was on the run. Robert fell, again to the dark queen. The King swore under his breath to slay her himself, but time was running out. Another pawn died, leaving the King in deadly check. He stumbled back, searching desperately for some escape. How could things have gone so bad so early? Bruce made one final attempt to help his King, but it was too late. The King found himself facing the black queen, unable to attack due to her bishop, or escape due to the battlefield's end. From his dark square, Bruce glared helplessly at the queen, who stood on a white square.

The black queen stared the King dead in the eye, and uttered the dreaded words.

"Checkmate."

The King could do nothing but concede. His army severely lacked in skill this time, but even as his Queen, Pawns, Bishops, Knights, and Rooks solemnly rose and lined up in their proper squares, the King knew that the next game would be invariably different.

Such was the nature of Chess.

CONNEXION

A *TRIUMVIRATE* STORY
(2006)

Note: The following story takes place approximately six months after the events depicted in the novel, Pandora's Game.

A slow, shallow breath. So weak, so *weary*, it made Lucius want to cry.

"... Gran ... dad ...?"

"Yeah?"

"... Granddad ...?"

"Yes, Travis, I'm here."

"I ... love you ... Granddad."

"Shh. Quiet now."

"... not ... not your fault ... my choice ... *my* choice ... love you ..."

Lucius had no reply for that. He reached out to touch the boy's hand ...

But there was an obstacle Lucius hadn't expected, though he probably should have by now. The white woman — the *witch doctor* woman, as far as Lucius was concerned — had already placed her damned hand on his grandson's before he could get there.

"Breathe deep, Travis" she told the young man, as though by merely *saying* that she would give power back to his failing lungs — *fool*! "Concentrate. Focus. It's not too late. Call your power, Travis ..."

Travis offered the feeblest of nods, closed his jaundice eyes, and tried to do just that. Lucius shook his head at this needless waste of time ... but he kept his counsel to himself.

Lucius' grandson was dying. And there was not a damned thing Lucius could do about it.

But see, *that* was the bitch of it. There *was* something that he could do ... if only the pigheaded boy would let him *do* it.

Travis — born Lucius Travis Bekele III of a proud African-American line — had leukemia. "Cancer of the blood," as it was sometimes called, but the doctors told Lucius that was kind of misleading. Travis' body was tearing itself apart, and while those same doctors had given him about a one-in-five chance of the operation working like they had hoped it might, they had given him *zero* chance without it.

Of course, now it was probably far too late, anyway ... no matter *what* that witch doctor said!

Travis needed a bone marrow transplant. But his parents were long in the grave, God rest their souls, and he had no siblings. His only living relative was Lucius ... eighty-seven-year-old, granddad Lucius.

Lucius himself wasn't in the best of health. Nothing specific was wrong with him, he was just ... old. And those same damned doctors had to go and be honest with the boy, and tell him that they feared for Lucius' being able to stand the bodily shock of the hip-pokin' donation process.

So then pigheaded Travis had to go and make a big stink about it. How he didn't want his granddad, who was the only "parent" he'd ever known, to risk himself for his sake. He refused to sign the right papers — in fact, he even had a friend (some "friend!") draw up his *own* papers on his computer at home that made the hospital liable if they dared proceed against his wishes.

So ... Lucius had to sit by like some helpless nobody and watch his sweet, foolish Travis — once such a big, burly, strong young man — get weaker and weaker while the search went on for some non-biologically-related donor.

Lucius tried to convince Travis that his old life had been long and good and it was over, that he had seen many wondrous things, from his move to America as a boy to his people finally getting real civil rights here to their serving directly under the President of the United States, that he *wanted* to give it up if it could help his grandson see even *one more day* on God's green earth.

Travis wouldn't budge.

So Lucius got some big ideas in his head and tried to make his *own* stink. He wrote letters to every African-American "somebody" he could think of, from Reverend Jessie Jackson to then-living Johnny Cochran. He tried to play the whole "race card," to angle that these stuck-up white doctors were only letting his grandson die because he was *black*. He knew damned well that it wasn't true, but he was desperate for somebody — *any*body — to help.

But, in the end, Travis' life wasn't deemed *political* enough to get Jackson's attention, and Cochran up and died himself before Lucius got a response.

So ... Lucius went about the painful business of watching Travis gradually melt away.

Not that Travis was going out without *any* fight, mind you. He took the standard treatments, for all the good they did. But it was when he was given less than three months to live that he got desperate enough to call in that witch doctor.

"She's *not* a 'witch doctor,' Granddad," Travis corrected him more than once. "She's a hypnotherapist." Whatever the hell *that* meant!

At first, Lucius thought that maybe he could use this as leverage, to prove that his grandson was no longer "of sound mind and body," and that he could finally *force* the doctors to take the bone marrow Travis needed from him. But, much to his shock and dismay, several of the doctors actually *endorsed* this foolish effort! "Mind over matter" and whatnot. Lucius had to wonder if the whole world had gone crazy and he just hadn't gotten the damned memo!

So this "Doctor" Kramer, this "hypnotherapist," came to visit his grandson for one hour each and every day, including weekends. She had him stare at a tiny electric light until Lucius himself just about fell asleep — he made sure he sat in on these sessions; oh, yes, this witch doctor wasn't getting his grandson alone, no sir! — and then she *talked* to him. That's it. She didn't give him pills, she didn't get him shots, and she sure as hell didn't give him bone marrow. She just *talked* to him. Like *that* was going to do a damned bit of good!

At first it was a bunch of real nonsense about Travis' bad cells being evil aliens and his good cells being heroes in spaceships. Or something like that. "Visualization," she called it. Giving Travis something metaphorical to represent his body's efforts to save itself. Lucius, for one, thought that was pretty damned silly, and even Travis couldn't really get into it — his grandson was never a fan of that science-fiction hooey. "Doctor" Kramer apologized, saying that many young men around Travis' age grew up on *Star Wars* and so drew strength from the analogy.

So then she switched to something that made a *little* more sense to Lucius, at least at first. Instead of the spaceship tripe, she spoke to him all about bringing in "a higher force," to pull power into his body from "the world beyond" to help give him strength. To Lucius, it seemed obvious that she was talking about God Almighty, and *that* he could understand.

But, as should have come as no surprise to Lucius, the

whole deal went south from there. Travis would sit — and, later, lie — on his hospital bed, breathing deeply as the woman spoke to him in her soft voice. And did she talk about the power of God? Did she talk about the love of Jesus Christ? No. She encouraged Travis to connect to "a kindred spirit," to seek help from his "spiritual twin." Whatever the hell *that* meant!

A choking gasp from Travis shook Lucius from his musing and grumbling. He leaned forward, oblivious to how his elderly neck and back cracked in protest.

"Travis? You all right, boy?"

Travis did not respond. His too-thin face was drawn in, his eyes squeezed shut as he fought a wave of nausea, or *pain*.

"Breathe deep, Travis ..." the witch doctor prattled on.

"He *can't* 'breathe deep' right now, you idiot! Can't you see that?"

"Doctor" Kramer did not respond, either.

Muttering to himself, Lucius reached for the call-button, but then stopped. Travis' nurse had already warned that she could not administer another shot until the top of the hour. That was still twenty-five minutes away.

Don't they see that it doesn't make a bit of difference now? Don't they see that my sweet Travis is dying? *Can't they make it as* painless *as possible for him?*

"Call on your strength, Travis," the idiot was saying in her lulling, droning, *maddening* voice. "Call on your spiritual twin. Call on *Trey*."

Lucius rolled his eyes, and he did it over-the-top enough to make sure that the woman saw him do it.

"Trey" was the name that Travis had eventually given to this "spiritual twin" of his. Why not? Travis was "the third" in his line, so "Trey" was a good fit, right? And according to his weakening and (as far as Lucius was concerned) increasingly delirious grandson, this "Trey" was a warrior of some kind, a champion who had overcome his own death to endlessly seek to prevent that of others.

As the weeks had passed, Travis was supposedly calling this "Trey" closer and closer so as to pull more and more strength from him. But — as came as *no* surprise to Lucius — it had not been working. As Travis fell nearer to death, Kramer had gotten more bold with her approach, using the idea of "Trey" less as a metaphor and more as though he were a literal being who might swoop right in and save the day.

Damned witch doctor.

Travis gasped again. This time, the wave wasn't passing. These episodes were getting longer and harsher each day, and each one broke Lucius' heart a little bit more.

"Call to Trey," the woman was ranting, "Trey is coming to help you. Can you see Trey, Travis? Can you see him?"

Lucius opened his mouth with the full intention of tearing into this woman once and for all.

"Yes ... I see him ... I *see* him ..."

Lucius closed his mouth with a soft *click* of his false teeth. Lord God help him, his boy had finally lost it.

"That's good, Travis. That's very, very good. Now, I want you to picture Trey coming closer to you, Travis. Trey is moving closer and closer—"

"All ... red ... ear ..."

"I'm sorry, Travis, I didn't hear you. What did you say?"

"Here ... he's already .... *here* ..."

"That's very good, Travis. Now, picture yourself reaching out—"

"Here ... *here* ..."

The woman looked just a little bit perplexed now.

Lucius asked, "What's the matter, 'Doctor'? Somethin'

you didn't expect?"

Kramer afforded him the briefest of glances. "It's not uncommon for the hypnotic imagery to take on a life of its own. Sometimes that's the surest sign that it's *working*. But..."

" 'But' *what?*"

"Here ..." Travis was muttering over and over again. His sunken eyes danced back and forth beneath their bruised-looking lids. "Here ... already here ..."

"I'm not sure," Kramer admitted at last. "Trey should be providing strength, or at least comfort by now. *Especially* if Travis believes they are now together. But he seems almost—"

"Here!" Travis suddenly burst much louder, causing both of his visitors to jolt in surprise. *"He's ... here!"*

The next sound did not exactly surprise Lucius, but it still filled him with despair.

The alarms blared. The alarms from all that hospital equipment wired into his grandson.

Travis' heart had stopped.

"Damn you, woman!" he bellowed, seizing Kramer none too gently by the wrist. "What did you *do*?!"

Before she could answer — if, indeed, she had any to offer — the door burst inward, and a river of medical staff flowed into Travis' room.

"Doctor Kramer, Mister Bekele," the physician in charge announced, "I'll have to ask you to step outside."

Lucius wanted to protest — oh, how he wanted to — but in the end, he was too smart for that. He'd seen enough T.V. dramas to know that if he argued or made a fuss, some big bully of an orderly would appear and just carry him out like a two-year-old.

And, to be honest, while a large part of him *did* want to be here if these were to be his grandson's last moments ...

another, selfish part had no particular desire to witness his undignified death.

Maybe they would even save Travis, for however much longer. But Lucius doubted it.

He suddenly realized that he was still holding the witch doctor's wrist. He shoved it — shoved her — away in disgust and vacated the room.

*   *   *

"Mister Bekele ...?"

Lucius jerked awake. He had been resting in a chair down the hall from Travis' room, trying not to listen to the hubbub that leaked from behind its closed door. As happened so often these days, he had dozed off without realizing it. Of course, this time he had to wonder: How much of it was age, and how much was his desire to escape the very news he knew was now forthcoming?

"Yes, sir," he acknowledged without bothering to stand.

"If you could please follow—"

"No need, sir. You ain't gonna surprise me. My grandson is *dead* now, isn't he?"

The tall, white man hesitated for a moment, perhaps suspicious of the old man's apparent resolve. How many brave souls had fallen to pieces when the word became official?

"Isn't he?" Lucius repeated without vehemence.

"Yes, sir. I'm afraid that he is."

Lucius nodded. The physician relaxed a bit.

Lucius had rehearsed this in his mind for days now. Travis had wanted to be cremated — all of *those* papers had been signed many months ago — so there wasn't much for Lucius to do now but thank the man for his troubles and leave. His grandson had offered words of love and of amnesty, then prattled on with that stupid woman about "Trey" for a few minutes, and then died. That was it. It was over. Nothing more for Lucius to do but to rise and go home.

Which is why Lucius was so surprised to hear himself say, "I'll want some time alone with him before you take him away."

"Of course, Mister Bekele."

"And I don't want to be rushed. He's being burned to ash, my Travis is. So you don't need to worry about making him all pretty or whatever."

"No, sir. That's the—"

"You best not be rushing me, now. I'll come out when I'm done, and I don't want you people bothering me any sooner, you understand me? And I want you to keep that 'hypnotherapist' bitch away from us. She's done enough ... which amounts to *nothin' at all*."

The doctor nodded his agreement to Lucius' terms.

Lucius himself nodded, and hoisted his stiffening body to its feet. He stretched as best he could, then took the first step back to see his boy.

But why? Wasn't the fading rot of the leukemia enough to witness? Why did he want to see Travis like *this*? He didn't know.

As he approached the room just as the final nurse made her exit, Lucius caught sight of "Doctor" Kramer from the corner of his eye.

I swear to you, God, if she comes over here right now, I'm gonna—

But it didn't come to that. Right or wrong, fair or unfair, Kramer must have read the anger and hostility in Lucius' body, because she thought better of whatever she might have said and instead turned to the bank of elevators.

Lucius nodded again, this time in satisfaction, and

closed Travis' door behind him.

*　　*　　*

They had covered Travis with a sheet.

Lucius pulled it away. He wanted to look at this grandson. He wanted to *see* his boy.

But *why*, damn it? This person did not look at all like the Travis he knew, the Travis he had raised and nurtured — as well as a man can — for over twenty years. This hollowed shell, with its sunken eyes and ashen skin, was an imposter to Lucius. An imposter who had taken his grandson away, because he had refused to accept a tired old man's bone marrow.

Lucius wiped his tears away before they had a chance to escape the rims of his eyes. No, this *was* his Travis, and he knew it. But now Travis belonged only to God, and if Lucius had been too cowardly to watch his actual passing — big orderlies or no, he *would* have stayed if he'd really wanted to, the hospital rules be damned! — then the least he could do was to usher his sweet Travis' soul into the afterlife.

Lucius eased himself into the same chair he had occupied during that stupid woman's final session. It had been shoved aside by the medical staff as they had struggled in vain to bring Travis back, and he left it where it had come to rest. Before, he'd angled it so as to keep an eye on that woman; now, as it turns out, he was a bit further away but found himself better facing Travis. That suited him just fine.

He closed his eyes, and began to pray ...

*　　*　　*

Lucius awoke when he heard movement.

He had nodded off again during his prayers (yeah, getting old was a difficult business, not for the weak of heart). On some half-awake level, he had been aware that it was happening, but this time it actually brought him a touch of peace. He was just sitting here, dozing away, in the presence of his grandson. He would never be able to do this again, not in this life, so ... so be it.

And now *someone* was moving around the room, and that rankled him something fierce.

"Damn it," he began even before his eyes were focused, "I told you people ..."

But there was no one else here.

"Huh," Lucius muttered, unaware that he had made the sound. He glanced at the clock, and found that very little time had actually passed. Between his prayers and his little half-nap, only ...

His thoughts stopped, as did his breath.

Travis' eyes were open.

They had been closed when he'd come back into the room — hell, they'd been closed when his heart had stopped. When Lucius had pulled away the sheet ... damn it, *they had been closed*.

And now they were open.

A chill ran down Lucius' spine.

Okay, all right ... there was an explanation for this. When a person dies with their eyes open, we'd all seen those movies where someone rubs them closed. What a lot of people did *not* realize was that they tended to open up again once the body started drying out and tightening up. One of Lucius' best friends back in the '70s had been an undertaker, and he had explained how they had to sew the eyelids shut so that folks at their open casket funerals didn't get an unexpected fright.

But how long did that usually take? Lucius did not

know. Travis had been dead for less than an hour, but ...

Indulging in a groan, Lucius pushed himself back to his feet. Shuffling forward, he moved to Travis' side. The young man's eyes were fixed and dilated.

And there was more, something he had not noticed at first, so distracted he was by the dead gaze: Travis' body seemed ... *bigger,* somehow. Not a lot, mind you. But ... well, the last time Travis had been weighed (a week or two ago, he thought), he had almost gotten down to some hundred-and-forty-odd pounds, and that was pretty damned thin for someone who stood over six-foot-four. Now, in death, Travis looked at least ten pounds heavier than he had in those last moments before Lucius had been ordered from the room.

It must be one of those things. Like with his eyes opening. There was a lot of swelling in a dead body. A little creepy, but no big deal, right?

The room seemed colder than before.

Should he close his grandson's eyes?

Lucius reached out to do just that, but then stopped himself short. Would Travis' skin already be cool to the touch? If so, did he really want to *feel* that? If Travis was already starting to bloat, then it might ...

All right, old man. You just settle down now. You chickened out of witnessing his passing, and now you're gonna leave his eyes open because you're too squeamish to feel his cold skin? You should be ashamed *of yourself!*

Again, this time with determination, he reached out to drag the eyelids down as they should be.

The eyes moved.

The dead boy looked right at him.

It was truly a wonder that Lucius did not drop dead of a heart attack right on the spot.

But Lucius did not drop dead. He *did,* however, gasp

— no, *whimpered* is more like it — and stumble away from the bed until his legs struck the chair and he collapsed onto his ass hard enough to bruise his tail bone.

With slow, awkward movements (but how can they be "awkward" when he's not supposed to be moving *at all?!*), Travis sat up in bed. It took much longer than it would have had he been ... "healthy" ... but at the same time, the motions were very *deliberate*, as though it were a much more complicated task which required a great deal of thought. His dry, glassy gaze never left Lucius, and there was now no doubt at all that his body had taken on additional mass since the time of his death.

"Ggaaa ..." came out of Travis' mouth, but Lucius had no idea if it were an attempt to speak or just an incidental noise from the apparent effort of sitting up.

"Sweet God in Heaven," Lucius whispered, his lips numb. "Help me, Lord ..."

Travis was still now. He merely sat there on the bed, staring at Lucius and appearing *not* to breathe.

Lucius wanted to run, but he was paralyzed below the neck. All he could do was continue appealing to God. "Our Father ... who art in Heaven ... hallowed be Thy Name ..."

Finally, Travis looked away. He peered downward, inspecting his hand. In the rush of trying to save his life, the medical staff had either forgotten or not bothered to remove the IV from the back of Travis' left hand. Travis reached over with his right and pulled the needle free, and without much care. There was very little blood, but he *did* bleed.

It struck Lucius now that perhaps this was all a mistake. Maybe Travis had not really died after all, but merely fallen into a coma. Of course, there were mounds of evidence *against* this unlikely theory, not the least of which was the fact that he *still* didn't look like he was breathing ... but then, what *else* was Lucius supposed to believe at this point?

Swallowing so hard that it hurt a little, he spoke, "Travis ...?"

His grandson did not respond. Even though the needle was long gone and the brief bleeding had already stopped, he was still enamored, for whatever reason, with the back of his left hand.

"Travis?" Lucius tried again. Should he call for help? What *else* should he do? Now, where did that damned call button go ...?

Whereas he had not responded to Lucius' voice, Travis *did* react when the old man shifted forward in his chair. His head wobbled slightly as he turned to regard his grandfather once more. He stared at Lucius, and now his gaze was not quite as vacant as before. There was a touch of ... something else. Was it recognition? Was this a miracle after all, and Lucius was just too damned jittery to recognize it?

All right now, old man. Let's not be too hard on yourself. The boy just came back from the dead, and he might have some magical weight back, but he still *don't look too good. If this* is *a resurrection, it ain't* clean *like Jesus Christ's. And besides, you know that look on his face ain't "recognition," don't you?*

No, Lucius supposed he knew that it was not. It was too primal for that. For all the world, he looked ...

"No," Lucius whispered. No, it couldn't be *that*.

Travis opened his mouth, and that "Ga!" sound came out again, but this time it was stronger, more willful. The boy, the *dead* boy, worked his dry lips and swallowed with his thick tongue and that look got stronger.

He looked ... he looked ...

Hungry.

Lucius was an intelligent man, but he had no more interest in horror movies than his grandson had in science-fiction. If asked to define the word *undead*, he would have assumed the person meant "not dead" and looked at them as though they were just being foolish.

But that did not prevent a vague acknowledgment of what such an expression on Travis' face might mean. His grandson, risen from the dead and not altogether right in the head ... regarding him with *hunger*? No, Lucius did not need to know about words like *zombie* to imagine that this did not bode well.

"Help me, Lord God," he prayed, "for I am most definitely walking through the valley of the shadow of *death...*"

He crept forward in his chair, and as before, the movement of his body excited his late grandson when his voice had not. Travis was leaning toward him now, and his thickening legs were making a sort of kicking motion.

He was trying to get out of the bed.

Lucius licked his cracked lips with an equally dry tongue. Travis seemed to be gaining coordination and mobility, but he was still very ungainly. Could Lucius make it to the door before Travis got close enough to reach him?

Did he have any choice but to try?

Tensing his aching muscles, Lucius prepared to make a run for it.

"Stay where you are, Mister Bekele. For your own safety, please do not move."

For the second time in as many minutes, Lucius felt that he was on the brink of a heart attack. Jerking his eyes away from his advancing grandson, Lucius found that they were no longer alone.

Despite the fact that the door *had not opened*, there was now a white man standing in the room with them. He was tall and slender and well-dressed and Lucius did not really care about any of that because he was too busy hoping that this mysterious stranger was going to *help him*!

"Please—" Lucius began.

"Do not move, Mister Bekele," the man repeated. *"And it would probably be best if you did not speak, either."*

Lucius answered with a quick nod, then turned himself into a statue.

The stranger's warning aside, Travis did not seem any more interested in the newcomer's voice than he had been in his grandfather's. His legs were hanging well over the edge of the bed now, his feet very nearly touching the floor. In moments, he would be standing, and moments after that ...

Lucius prayed.

The stranger took a step forward. This slight movement did not seem enough to draw Travis' hungry eyes away from the old man, so next the stranger clapped his hands together. Only once, but it made a sharp sound in the little room.

That did it. Travis finally shifted his gaze away from Lucius, settling after a couple of seconds on the white man. His lips peeled back in affectation of a snarl or growl, but the only noise he made, yet again, was "Ga!"

Heedless of any possible threat, the man took another step forward, closing the distance between them to a degree that made *Lucius* nervous. Once Travis was on his feet, it would take very little motion to get the stranger within grabbing range.

The stranger did not seem concerned in the least. He cocked his head to one side, as though he were studying Travis, or perhaps contemplating his next move. Whatever it was, Lucius hoped that he would make it in a hurry!

"I find myself questioning," he said at last, though Lucius was not sure at first to whom he was speaking, *"what exactly is the best way to proceed? You are not quite like Sean and me and you never have been, nor has your crossover been executed in quite the same fashion ..."*

Lucius had been too stunned, and scared, to notice before, but now it struck him: This white man had a *strange* voice. It was something ... something in the tone? The accent? *What* accent? Lucius wasn't sure. He wasn't sure of *anything* anymore.

"... we both," the man was saying, *"experienced a difficult transitional period. I can only hope that you will be able to endure your own ..."*

With one last, cumbrous shove, Travis was on his feet. He afforded Lucius a (thankfully) brief glance, but his attention had clearly shifted focus.

"... for if you do not ... then we cannot allow you to continue as you are. Do you understand?"

Travis made that snarl-face again.

"Does any *part of you understand me, Trey?"*

Trey! *That* got Lucius' attention in a heartbeat. Did this man, this stranger upon whom he had never before laid eyes, just call his grandson "Trey?"

That woman! That damned, *damned* witch doctor! *She* had something to do with this! That was the only explanation!

In spite of the outlandish circumstances before him, Lucius found himself preparing to bolt to his feet and demand an explanation from this invasive white man.

"Mister Bekele," the man said without taking his eyes off Travis, *"this would* not *be the best time."*

Lucius kept his peace.

The stranger and Travis continued their little staring contest. Lucius could no longer see his grandson's dried out eyes all that well — he was standing in profile from Lucius' point of view — but he could see the stranger's just fine. And just as with his voice, Lucius now realized there was something not quite right with his eyes.

He hasn't blinked, Lucius deduced with some

satisfaction. *I don't think he's blinked once since he ... "walked" in here? Just where in the hell did this bastard come from?!*

The two stood rock still for several more seconds before Travis released another "Ga!" ...

... and lunged for the white man.

Even with some of his natural mass returned to him — there seemed to be even more now than when Lucius first noticed the difference — Travis was nowhere near his pre-leukemia self. That considered, Travis was still a good four inches taller than the slender stranger, still the huskier of the two.

But the white man made no attempt to avoid Travis' attack. He spread his arms to his sides, encouraging Travis to wrap him up in a sort of bear hug-tackle. The momentum carried them back a couple of steps, halting just before they would have collided with the closed door.

Travis opened his mouth wide and made as though — God forbid this sight! — he intended to *bite* the stranger. The white man reached up and brought his hands together, seizing Travis by either side of his face. With surprising strength, the man not only kept Travis' mouth away from his person, but forced the biting dead man to return his gaze once more.

"Listen to me, Trey," he said, *"I am sorry that we must do this in so harsh a manner. But after the havoc we have already caused in this world, to the lives of Carpenter and Hudson, we cannot indulge ourselves in allowing you to run rampant."*

"Ga!" was all Travis had to say to that. The cords of his neck stood out in his effort to snap forward and bite the man's face off.

But still the stranger held him back. And there was more.

As he held Travis' face so tight, the stranger's blue eyes began to ... fade? Shrink? Lucius could not be sure. The whites of his eyes appeared to "bleed" into the center, until the man had first no irises, then no pupils.

And what's more, once *that* whole business — which took maybe three seconds, give or take — was complete ... *then* those all-white eyes turned iridescent. It was halfway between glowing on their own and reflecting the lights within the room like a rat's might. It was the damnedest thing Lucius had ever seen.

Well ... except seeing his grandson come back from the dead, that is.

Now that the man's eyes had gone inhuman, which was the only word to describe it, Travis was reacting a little more. At first he looked like he might calm down, but then he started fighting *harder*, making that "Ga! Ga! Ga!" sound with more frequency and intensity.

Whatever the man was doing to him with those white eyes, Travis didn't like it. For a moment, Lucius felt protective anger on the part of his grandson, but it didn't last. Again, Lucius was not a stupid man.

"Listen to me, Trey Matthews," the man said, and that whatever-quality to his voice was stronger than ever, *"you have made the crossover. You have followed Sean and me, and you have done it without commandeering an innocent life."* Then, in a lower tone and a touch of regret, he added, *"Would it were that we had been so fortunate."*

Travis struggled; Lucius watched.

"You are better than this, Trey. You are stronger than this. You proved it once before. Now you must prove it again."

Travis was really fighting now. He was no longer trying to bite the man, but now simply to pull away and escape his grasp, and those eyes. Those white eyes were *definitely* glowing now, and it was making it difficult even for Lucius to look at them.

"Come to me, Trey Matthews. Come to me now.*"*

Lucius looked away. Those eyes were becoming too disturbing, and *not* simply because no man should *have* eyes like that. There was *more* in them, something powerful and commanding, which threatened to overwhelm Lucius even though he was not the target of that power.

What should he do now, anyway? *However* he was managing it, the stranger was holding Travis, so for the time being, Lucius did not appear to be in any immediate danger. Should he try to slip past them and out the door? No, there wasn't enough room to pull that off. Should he try to find that call-button for the nurse after all? Or what about the phone? Where had the phone gotten to ...?

As he looked around the room, Lucius just happened to catch a glimpse of the large, fisheye mirror in the far, upper corner by the door. All it took was that quick glance to seize his undivided attention.

Dear God in Heaven ...

In that round mirror, Lucius could see a warped reflection of the entire room. He could see the hospital bed and all of that equipment and machinery. He could see himself, looking older than Moses. And he could see his dead grandson Travis, standing a few feet from the door and struggling.

Struggling with *nothing*.

Dear God in Heaven, the strange white man holding his grandson at bay *did not cast a reflection*. And maybe Lucius didn't know about words like "undead," but in twenty-first-century America, an old man would have to be far more sheltered than Lucius to not know what *that* meant.

Lucius crossed himself with a trembling hand ... and wished to God that he had a real one in his hand right now.

"Come to me, Trey," the man — the *vampire* — was saying, *"come to me ..."*

With a degree of cunning he had not displayed since his "reawakening," Travis shifted his weight to one side, and then suddenly threw himself to the other. It caught the white man unprepared, and Travis slipped free.

Travis teetered off balance, spun around ... and staggered straight toward Lucius.

"Ga!" he shouted in delight, like an obese man finding a pastry he had almost forgotten. The stranger dismissed, he reached for his grandfather, his teeth bared.

Paralyzed, Lucius could only whisper, "Travis ..."

What happened next occurred in slow-motion to Lucius, though he later realized that it must have actually happened in the blink of an eye. Travis' hands were reaching out, clutching at him, clutching for his throat. His mouth opened wider in anticipation, and Lucius saw in horrible, graphic detail how the corners of his lips cracked and split — they were too dry in death to accommodate such facial movement. His eyes widened, their surfaces now looking milky, not unlike the thickening cataract over Lucius' own left eye. His hands reaching, reaching, reaching ...

Then, between them, an impossible cloud of ivory vapor condensed from translucent to opaque faster than Lucius could follow even in "slow-motion." Faster than thought — hell, faster than *light*, as far as Lucius could tell — the mist solidified into a person, the strange white man, the vampire, now stood between him and his savage grandson.

The vampire struck Travis in a crude but effective uppercut, killing Travis' forward momentum. And before Travis could recover, he had not only seized Travis by the face once more, but had forced the larger man down to the floor in a clumsy genuflection. Travis' hospital gown split up the middle as his long legs spread it too wide. Maybe it showed his privates to the world, maybe it didn't — Lucius didn't look.

"That is enough, *Trey. We do not have the luxury of dealing with this gently."*

With his back turned, Lucius could no longer see the vampire's eyes, but he could *sense* that their power was stronger than ever. He *could* see Travis' eyes now, and for the first time, they held something akin to *fear*.

"You will either find yourself and come to me ... or I will be forced to end *this."*

Now Travis was even *breathing* like a living person again, and his exhalations were heaving gasps. His milky eyes widened, and he looked like a drowning man, desperate in his desire to be saved.

"Ga ... ga ..."

Lucius heard the vampire say, *"Bitte, G-G-Gott, gib ihm die Kraft, zur Vernunft zu kommen,"* under his breath (was that Yiddish? German?), then he raised his voice and added, *"Now, Trey. Now, or never."*

Travis' whole body trembled under some monumental effort.

Lucius held his own breath, in anticipation of ... what? He did not know, could not name it, but he felt how important, how *critical*, it was.

"Ga! ... Ga! ..."

The energy in the room was thick. Lucius could feel it on his skin, in his bones, in his mind.

"Ga! ... Ga! ... Ga! ..."

Then, just like that, Travis relaxed. He blinked, though his eyes were so dry, the lids only closed halfway.

"Ga .. Gaaaayle?"

The stranger sighed and loosened his own posture somewhat. His strong, gripping hands stopped squeezing Travis' face and instead *stroked* his cheeks with affection.

"Vielen Dank, lieber G-Gott," he said, again under his breath but not so low that Lucius could not hear it (and this time Lucius was pretty sure it was German). Then, *"No, Trey. I am afraid that your sister is not here. I cannot even say* when *you might see her again. I am sorry."*

Travis clearly didn't *like* that, but he did not react in anger, merely poignant disappointment. With improved coordination, and the vampire's help, Travis stood and moved to the bed. He sat on the edge, his long, still-thickening legs draped down to the floor ... and found fascination once again with the small wound left by the IV on the back of his hand.

The vampire turned to Lucius, and thank God, his eyes were back to their normal blue. Maybe they didn't blink, and maybe they still seemed to stare straight through to the back of Lucius' head ... but at least they *looked* human again.

Not that Lucius was fooled. Between glowing eyes, missing reflections, and turning into smoke, this man was about as "human" as ... as ... well, whatever.

"I apologize for arriving late, Mister Bekele. As I know you have guessed, I had to wait until after dark. My partner, Sean, was willing to come on his own, but he lacked the ability to convey Trey across the bridge."

" 'Convey' ... 'bridge' ... Mister, I have no idea *what* you are talkin' about."

The man's face suggested a smile of bemusement without actually changing expression. *"Yes, of course. Forgive me."* He offered his hand. *"My name is Alistaire Bachman."*

Lucius stared at the offered hand. "You'll, ah ... you'll have to excuse me if I ain't comfortable shaking with you."

Whereas before Bachman had hinted at bemusement, now he whispered of regret and sad understanding — again, all without appearing to move a single facial muscle. *"Yes.*

Of course." He lowered his hand.

"What's happened to my grandson?" Lucius demanded. "What's been done to him?"

"*Mister Bekele,*" Bachman said, "*you're grandson, Travis, is dead.*"

"Just like that, huh?" Lucius snapped. "So who is *that* sittin' there on the bed, huh?"

"*That, Mister Bekele, is no longer your grandson. His name is Trey Matthews—*"

"Yeah, 'Trey,' I know *all* about 'Trey,' Mister Bachman. And I suppose you're gonna tell me you don't work with a woman by the name of 'Doctor' Kramer?"

"*No, Mister Bekele, I do not.*"

Lucius guffawed.

"*Sean and I have been aware of Doctor Kramer for a short time now, but she is unaware of us.*"

"Is that a fact?"

"*Yes, that is a fact.*"

Lucius rolled his eyes and stood. Stepping around Bachman, his immediate impulse was to move protectively to Travis' side ... but then he hesitated.

"*I do not believe Trey will harm you, Mister Bekele, now that he is fully here. Trey has always displayed remarkable fortitude — at times, I have envied him. It was the transitional period that was hardest on us all.*"

"Is that so?" But Lucius was only listening with half-an-ear now. Cautiously, he moved to the side of the bed. Travis looked up, and that expression of hunger was, thankfully, absent. But neither was there recognition. "Travis?" Nothing.

"*Were he more like us,*" Bachman explained as though Lucius had asked, "*there would be residual memories. With Sean and—*"

"I ain't interested." As casually as he could manage,

Lucius reached over to the little table of supplies next to Travis' bed. He picked up one tongue depressor, then another one.

"I am merely trying to explain, Mister Bekele. You're grandson was a dying man. I find it fair to say that, even if you had *been able to give him your bone marrow, he still would not have survived. But I want you to know that something noble, something* good *will come of his death."*

"Is that a fact?" Lucius prompted, keeping his back to the vampire.

"Yes, sir, it is. My partner and I wage war against other creatures *such as ourselves."*

"Do ya?"

"Yes, we do. And for a few years now, Trey Matthews has been a part of that war. But you see, we are not ... from here."

A dry chuckle. "Is that so? Well, ya coulda fooled me."

"That is not exactly what I mean, Mister Bekele. Sean, Trey, and I—"

Lucius whirled as fast as he could. He raised the two tongue depressors in a single hand, his fingers holding them together in the shape of a cross.

"Get *back*, you spawn of Satan!"

Bachman flinched visibly, but he did not cower from the religious symbol as Lucius had hoped. *"Mister Bekele, please ..."*

"Get *back*, I said!" Lucius took a step forward. Bachman retreated a matching step, and that gave Lucius hope. "Maybe you saved my life just now and maybe you didn't. But you are *not* going to harm my grandson any more than you and that foolish woman already have. I don't know *what* he is now, but *he* still casts a reflection in that there mirror, so that sure as hell makes him different from *you!"*

Lucius brandished the makeshift cross higher, with more force. Bachman flinched again, but he did not retreat further.

"You misunderstand, Mister Bekele. Neither I, nor Doctor Kramer, have harmed your grandson in any—"

"Bullshit, sir. God forgive my language."

"G-God, " Bachman said in a choking voice, and Lucius realized that he had stuttered much the same way when he had spoken in German earlier. *"Yes, let us talk about G-God ... together."*

Lucius opened his mouth to retort, but then said nothing. He wasn't sure *what* to say to that. Weren't these things supposed to ... what? Hiss and run away or something when you shoved a cross in their face? Maybe because it wasn't a real one ...

The hospital door opened.

"Help!" Lucius cried. "You gotta ... help ..."

The man who entered was not dressed like a doctor — the new white man wore nothing but jeans and a tight T-shirt. He had opened the door just wide enough to step inside, and then he closed it behind him. Lucius immediately got the sense that this was *not* the cavalry.

"Ye all right, Alistaire?" the man asked in a thick Irish accent — what was this, a European convention?!

"Yes, Sean. I am fine."

"Ye want me to take it from him?" 'Sean' asked, nodding toward Lucius' improvised cross.

"No, Sean. Allow Mister Bekele to keep it. If he feels safer, perhaps he will be more inclined to listen."

"Yeah," Lucius spat, "I wouldn't count on *that* too much. And you," he demanded of Sean, "I suppose *you* are in on this, too, huh?"

"That would depend on what ye mean by 'in on this,'

Mister Bekele. But aye, I am here with Alistaire to collect Trey."

"*Travis*! Damn it, his - name - is - *Travis*!"

Lucius' hand shook with vehemence ... a little too *much* vehemence, as it turned out. His fingers slipped, and while the wooden depressors did not fall from his grasp, they shifted out of place, losing the shape of the cross almost entirely.

Lucius gasped and stumbled back against the supply table, struggling to reassemble his cross before the vampire (the *two* vampires?) could descend upon him ...

Neither Bachman nor his associate made any move against Lucius. Bachman relaxed slightly when the cross fell apart, but that was all.

Still, Lucius put his symbol back together as quickly as he could. He just didn't advance as far or shove it in Bachman's face this time.

"My grandson — *Travis* — and I are leavin'. I don't know what's wrong with him, but I'm guessin' that maybe he ain't dead after all. Maybe the doctors can still help him ..."

Sean looked down at the floor, his brown eyes sad. Bachman merely stood there, allowing Lucius to say his fill.

"We're leavin' this room, together. Now, I want you two to stand aside— Ah!"

A hand touched Lucius' shoulder, causing him to cry out. Good Lord, was there *another* one ...?!

But it was Travis who had touched him. A gentle touch, but still unnerving given his recent behavior. Yet there was no sign of that snarling, hungry animal now; his dry, milky eyes were, if anything, gentle.

"G ... g ... grann ... dad?"

Lucius' mouth hung open, and his eyes beamed with joy. He turned back to Bachman and the other, and though he said nothing in words, his expression was clearly one of

You See! Take that!

"Alistaire ...?" Sean asked, uncertain.

Bachman, too, appeared quite surprised. *"I believe, Sean, that we have once again underestimated Trey's mental capacity. You would think that we would have learned by now."*

Now Lucius *did* say, "You see? You see?! He *is* still my grandson! None of this 'Trey Matthews' nonsense—!"

"N-nno, gran-dad," Travis said, pulling Lucius' attention back around. "I-I ... am Tra-vis ... *and* Trey. Trey. Tra-vis. Trey."

Lucius stared. He shook his head in denial. "No. *No*, Travis. You're not ... you're ..."

The cross fell apart again, and this time the two sticks slipped from his hand, one landing on the bed and one tumbling to the floor. What difference did it make? His grandson was either still sick and brainwashed ... or dead, and gone to him. Either way, what did it matter? Lucius had accepted Jesus Christ as his Lord and Savior many years ago. These vampires could take his life, but that was all.

But the two still did not advance. At least, not together and not in force.

With a gesture for Sean to remain, Bachman crept forward with patience and care — so as not to appear "threatening" was Lucius' guess. When he drew very close, Travis turned to look at him.

"Alll ... istaire?"

"Yes, Trey."

"I ... member you ... and Sean. I member ... Gayle. But ... I member Grandad, too."

"Yes, Trey. That is how this world works. We come into this world, these people, and we keep many of these memories."

Travis nodded, then turned back to Lucius.

"Gran-dad."

"Yeah," Lucius choked, swallowing his tears.

"Grandad?"

"Yes, Travis, I hear you."

"I ... love you ... Grandad."

Lucius shivered with overwhelming deja vu, but said nothing.

"But ... I have to go."

Now Lucius looked his grandson straight in the eye, and his flowing tears be damned. "Must you, Travis? *Must* you?"

"Yeah ... I must ... Grandad."

"Mister Bekele," Bachman said in a soft voice, that "weird" quality stepping down a notch or two, *"if you like, we could try to contact you once we have—"*

"No, no, no. If you're gonna take my boy, just *take* him and be done with it, damn you."

"Mister Bekele—"

"Just *go!*"

Bachman nodded to Lucius, then turned and nodded to Sean. The Irishman popped off a half-salute and slipped out of the room — in spite of his sorrow and defeat, Lucius could not help noticing that the man was untucking his T-shirt as he disappeared. A small part of him wondered what in the world *that* was about, but mostly, he did not care.

With a helping hand from Bachman, Travis rose again from the bed. Lucius turned away, found the chair, and took what felt like years lowering himself into it.

"Mister Bekele," Bachman said, *"if you should happen to change your mind—"*

"I won't," Lucius whispered.

"But if you do *... I will attempt to contact you one month from now at your home. If you* still *do not wish to know and understand the G-God-given mission your*

grandson has allowed Trey to continue, then so be it. But if you wish to listen ... I will explain everything to you."

Lucius waved him away. He was tired, so tired.

"Your grandson's disappearance will cause a disturbance—"

Lucius guffawed, his sarcasm clear in that sound.

"I respectfully suggest that you leave shortly after us and plea ignorance on the matter."

"Somehow I don't think just my sayin' 'I don't know' about a missing body will be enough."

"Perhaps not. But ... the staff of this hospital will have many *other issues on their minds after tonight."*

"What do you—?"

At that moment, a tremendous racket erupted from outside the room. Lucius heard shouting and screaming and the sound of large equipment being knocked around or dropped. And then, topping it all, an immense roar — let's face it, a *howl*, just like a *wolf* — echoed throughout the entire building.

"Once Sean is finished," Bachman assured him, *"there will be so much confusion, they* might *not even ask you about your grandson's missing corpse."*

"So you've *maybe* covered the authorities. So what? What about Travis' friends? His co-workers? My neighbors?"

"Travis wished to be cremated, did he not*?"*

After a moment, Lucius reluctantly admitted, "Yes."

"And did he not already purchase his urn—"

"All right, all right. I get the picture."

Bachman nodded. He clearly wanted to say more, but wisely decided against it. He gestured Travis forward, opening the door for him. The noise outside grew louder, and Lucius was frustrated to admit that Bachman might have been correct about the confusion of the evening.

Travis looked back at him one more time and waved.

Lucius gritted his teeth and waved back.

Then they were gone.

For several long, long minutes, Lucius sat alone in the little room. The ruckus from outside faded, then grew louder, then faded again. So many thoughts ran through Lucius' mind, he couldn't keep track of them. All in all, he figured he was composing himself quite well. After all, in a matter of hours, he had lost his only grandson, seen him come back from the dead, discovered that vampires were real, and watched said vampire take his somewhat-resurrected grandson off to fight in a Holy War, or some such.

Yeah, under the circumstances, Lucius figured he was holding up just fine.

A sudden impulse pulled him, creaking and cracking, to his feet. He ambled over to the window and pulled the blinds all the way up. The lights in the room made it a little hard to see outside, but the parking lot area was well lit, so he did just fine with his good right eye.

People were running everywhere. Doctors, orderlies, patients. No one seemed hurt, thank God, but there was a lot of hysteria down there. Yeah, that Bachman bastard might have known what he was talking about after all.

And then he saw them. Bachman and the Irishman, with Travis walking between them — Travis' stride was surer than ever, so he did not appear to really *need* their help. Lucius watched the trio move toward the shadows at the far side of the parking lot, quickly but not running.

Just before they vanished from sight, they stopped. Travis turned around, and for a moment, Lucius thought he was actually looking up at him. Any doubts dissolved a moment later when Travis again waved at him, big and long.

This time, Lucius waved back to him with much more

feeling. He even raised his other hand to his lips and blew his grandson a kiss. Even from this height and distance, Lucius could see that Travis liked that very much.

And then they were gone.

Maybe. Maybe when Bachman called in one month — assuming he kept his word, but somehow Lucius suspected that he just might — maybe Lucius would do more than just hang up on him. Maybe he *would* listen, and ask questions about this little crusade of which Travis, or Trey, was a part.

Maybe. Who knows?

Stranger things had happened.

About the Author

CHRISTOPHER ANDREWS has been writing since the age of seven. While attending the University of Oklahoma, he completed two novels, *Refuge Among the Stars* (1989) and *The Blue Man* (1991), and a series of short-stories. In 1992, he co-created and wrote the premiere issue of the comic book *The Triumvirate*, and sold his first screenplay, "Thirst," to RF Video Productions.

In May of 1992, Christopher received a Bachelor's Degree in Theatre, and that August he traveled to California to pursue a career in acting — and he continued to write. In 1994, he co-plotted and scripted the premiere of Derek Lipscomb's comic book, *The Golden Scarab*, for Sharp Eye Graphix. In 1995, he co-wrote the science-fiction screenplay, *Dream Parlor*, with Jonathan Lawrence.

In 1999, he completed and published his third novel, *Pandora's Game*. And the *Dream Parlor* movie — in which he starred — premiered.

Over the next few years, Christopher completed and published three more novels: *Dream Parlor* (2000), the novelization of the film; *Paranormals* (2002); and *Hamlet: Prince of Denmark* (2005), the novelization of Shakespeare's play. And his short-stories "Mistake" and "Thirst" were adapted into short-films in 2004 and 2005, respectively.

Today, Christopher lives in California with his wife, Yvonne Isaak-Andrews. He is working on his seventh novel, *Of Wolf and Man*, the long-awaited sequel to *Pandora's Game*, and continues to work as an actor — *Dream Parlor* the movie is now available on DVD, and his next feature-film starring role, *Drivetime of the Dead*, is in post-production.

Excerpts from all of Christopher's novels can be found at www.dreamparlor.com.

www.ingramcontent.com/pod-product-compliance
Lightning Source LLC
Chambersburg PA
CBHW030214130726
47898CB00012B/1015